"I can't breathe," Melissa said, but she still didn't move away.

Miles was having a difficult time breathing himself and the temperature seemed to have shot up. She had that effect on him.

Then he realized the breathlessness they were feeling wasn't from the kiss.

Smoke filled the hayloft from the trapdoor they'd used to climb up. He ran to it and glanced down into the barn. Fire blazed upward, consuming the ladder as the horses, still in their stalls, whinnied and kicked, trying to escape the flames.

In the distance, footsteps rushed toward the barn and he recognized his brothers' voices as they started opening stalls and forcing out the animals.

He pushed her away from the opening as flames shot up and the ladder finally caved, crashing to the floor. "We can't get out that way."

Panic filled Melissa's face and he suspected she was thinking about Dylan and never seeing him again. He took her shoulders and locked eyes with her. "We'll figure out how to get out of here. I promise."

Virginia Vaughan is a born-and-raised Mississippi girl. She is blessed to come from a large Southern family, and her fondest memories include listening to stories recounted around the dinner table. She was a lover of books from a young age, devouring tales of romance, danger and love. She soon started writing them herself. You can connect with Virginia through her website, virginiavaughanonline.com, or through the publisher.

Books by Virginia Vaughan

Love Inspired Suspense

Cowboy Lawmen

Texas Twin Abduction
Texas Holiday Hideout

Covert Operatives

Cold Case Cover-Up
Deadly Christmas Duty
Risky Return
Killer Insight

Visit the Author Profile page
at Harlequin.com for more titles.

TEXAS HOLIDAY HIDEOUT

VIRGINIA VAUGHAN

LOVE INSPIRED SUSPENSE
INSPIRATIONAL ROMANCE

LOVE INSPIRED® SUSPENSE
INSPIRATIONAL ROMANCE

Recycling programs
for this product may
not exist in your area.

ISBN-13: 978-1-335-40312-4

Texas Holiday Hideout

Copyright © 2020 by Virginia Vaughan

This edition published by arrangement with Harlequin Books S.A.

For questions and comments about the quality of this book, please contact us
at CustomerService@Harlequin.com.

Love Inspired
22 Adelaide St. West, 40th Floor
Toronto, Ontario M5H 4E3, Canada
www.Harlequin.com

Printed in U.S.A.

For I know the thoughts that I think toward you, saith the Lord, thoughts of peace, and not of evil, to give you an expected end.

–Jeremiah 29:11

To the unknown little one who will be arriving around the same time as this book releases and changing my life for the better. Though I haven't yet seen your face, you are already precious to me and well worth the wait. I cannot wait to meet you.

ONE

Melissa Morgan carried her three-year-old son, Dylan, as they exited the car, following the US Marshals who led them through the hotel kitchen and up the elevator to the sixth floor. Surrounded by men with guns, the widowed single mom was still reeling from all that had happened. The Christmas music playing on the overhead speakers in the elevator only intensified her feeling that her life had become incredibly surreal over the past three weeks.

Dylan's presents had already been bought and wrapped and were sitting under their tree at home, never to be opened, never to be played with. The thought left her with an odd pang of sadness, but she couldn't really process it—not when she was still struggling with grief over her murdered mother, and shock over the revelations that had followed that death.

It wasn't until Melissa had walked in on the killer, a man the US Marshals insisted was tied to a mob boss, that she'd learned her mother had testified against that Mafia leader twenty years earlier, prompting them to enter the witness protection program. Melissa had been raised in the witness protection program. Her entire life was a lie. And up until three weeks ago, she'd had no idea.

It was all too much and now all of this had placed her and her son in danger.

Why didn't you ever tell me, Mama?

She felt hurt and angry at the secrets—but her questions about her mother and their past had to take a back seat for now while she dealt with the problems of the present. Most notably her mother's killer. The man she'd seen. The man she had identified, who was tied to the same crime web that had sent her mother into hiding years ago.

Melissa could never forget the face of the man who'd killed her mother, then turned the gun on her. She'd run for her life and been fortunate to escape, but now her life and her son's life were in danger.

The lead marshal stopped in front of a hotel-room door and opened it before ushering her inside. She put Dylan, who was still sleeping in her arms, onto the bed and covered him up. She placed a gentle kiss on his cheek, thankful for a child who slept through almost anything. He'd been a trouper through all of this, handling it all even better than she was. Of course, to him, this seemed like an adventure, but he'd still been remarkably brave and unselfish, rarely complaining that he missed his toys and his bedroom and, most of all, his gramma.

I miss her, too.

Two marshals remained outside the door while the

third, the one in charge, started securing the room. He checked the curtains and locks before turning to her.

"One of us will be outside the door at all times. All you need to do is call out if you need us."

She nodded and thanked him. "How long will I be here?"

"We have no way of knowing that, ma'am. I was just assigned to bring you here. My boss will designate a permanent marshal, who'll be in charge of your relocation." He eyed her neck in a manner that made her uncomfortable. She reached up and touched the necklace her mother had given her for her twenty-fifth birthday, a heart-shaped charm that she never took off.

"You were made aware that you can't keep anything from your previous life, weren't you?"

She touched her necklace again and gulped at his implication. "My mother gave me this necklace. It's all I have left of her."

"I understand, but it's also something that can tie you back to your past life."

She unlatched the chain and let the necklace fall into his hand, tears pressing against her eyes at the thought of severing her last tie to her old life and her mother. She hated to let the man see her cry, but she'd given up so many things already and this just seemed too much. "Excuse me," she said, pushing past him and rushing into the bathroom as tears slipped from her eyes.

She closed the door and locked it. He was only doing his job and she knew that, but it hurt losing that necklace. It poked right at the sore part of her heart that ached from losing her mother. She splashed water on her face and tried to pull herself together. She had to be strong for Dylan's sake. She couldn't allow these bad men, whoever they were, to get anywhere near him. She had to think about him instead of herself now. He deserved better than this, better than being shuttled between second-rate hotels from town to town, but she'd put up with this and anything else it took in order to keep him safe.

She checked herself in the mirror before walking back into the room. The marshal stood and she saw remorse on his face.

"I'm okay," she assured him. "It's just…it's a lot."

"I do understand that, ma'am." He held out the necklace to her and motioned for her to take it back. "I shouldn't be doing this," he admitted. "But I guess it won't do any harm to let you hold on to it. Just promise me you won't wear it. If any of the other marshals see it, they'll confiscate it."

Relief and gratitude filled her at his kind gesture. She took the necklace and slipped it into her pocket. "You're very kind. Thank you. And I promise."

He picked up the room-service menu and held it out to her. "Should I order something for you and your son?"

She glanced at Dylan, still asleep on the bed. "Not right now."

He nodded. "Then you should probably get some sleep. There's no telling when your new marshal will arrive."

She slipped off her shoes and crawled onto the bed. From between the drawn curtains, she caught a glimmer of the Christmas lights decorating the downtown area of whatever town she was in. She pulled Dylan into her arms and tried to calm herself enough to sleep as she heard the click of the door as the marshal slipped from the room.

There would be no Christmas for her and Dylan this year. And no Christmas with her mom ever again. But there *would* be Christmases to come for her son, if she could just get the two of them through this.

God, please watch over us and keep us safe.

She stroked her son's hair as she lifted up prayers for their safety and for God to give her strength to endure this nightmare.

WITSEC Inspector Deputy Marshal Miles Avery parked his SUV in the basement garage then entered the hotel lobby and spotted his boss waiting for him. Deputy Director Griffin Sheffield stood as Miles approached and reached for his hand.

"It's good to see you, Miles. It's been a while."

Miles had spent six weeks at his family's ranch in Texas over the summer after his father suffered a heart attack, then another several weeks providing around-the-clock security to a witness during an out-of-state trial so he and his boss hadn't been face-to-face for more than a few hours in quite a while. But his dad was now on the mend, the trial was over, and Miles was anxious to get back to a normal routine with the United States Marshals Service. "It's good to see you, Griffin. What do we have?"

Griffin handed him a file and Miles flipped through

it as his boss explained his current assignment. "Sixteen days ago, a WITSEC client was murdered in her home. Her daughter witnessed it. Thankfully, she escaped, but she identified the killer from a mug shot. His name is Richard Kirby. He's a known associate of Max Shearer, a mob boss the client helped put away. Shearer has just been granted a new trial by the courts and our victim was supposed to be the prosecution's main witness."

Miles understood the implication. "Now the daughter can tie him to this killing and witness tampering."

"Exactly. And Kirby managed to get away before the police or the marshals arrived. Our intel says he's gone into deep hiding for fear of being arrested, but that doesn't mean the threat against Melissa is over. Shearer still has dangerous men on his payroll. We immediately took Melissa and her son into protective custody, only we've had compromises in her security. We've been forced to move her three times."

"Is she breaking protocol?"

"We can't find any evidence that she is. That leads me to only one conclusion—we might have a leak in the US Marshals Service."

He stared at his boss, hoping he was pulling his leg, but the man's expression was dead serious. "A leak? How is that possible?" He couldn't believe anyone who signed up to protect witnesses would turn on one of them.

"I don't know, but we can't take any more risks with her safety. Now, I trust all my deputies, but you've been away for a while so I know for certain that you're not the leak. That's why I'm handing her and her son's protection over to you. Report directly to me, but otherwise keep any information about this case quiet from the other marshals. I had her and her son brought here late last night. No one's going to know that you're on this case. I'm going to tell everyone that your father took a turn for the worse and you've gone back home to care for him. That'll explain your absence from the office."

Part of his job was keeping secrets in order to protect witnesses, but he didn't like keeping secrets from his friends. He trusted them all, especially his partner, Lanie, and best friend, Adam. Because of the necessary restriction of information surrounding his job, they were the only people he could share his work life with. It was that kind of secrecy that had caused his last girlfriend to end their relationship, forcing him to accept the truth that he might never have the family he so desperately desired. But if his boss was correct and there was a leak in WITSEC, he couldn't take any chances with this witness's safety. He had to keep this assignment a secret from everyone—even those he was closest to.

He assured Griffin he would do his best, then walked upstairs with him to meet his new charge. She turned out to be a pretty, young woman with brown hair and sad eyes. She was doing her best to rein in a rambunctious little boy with the same dark eyes as hers.

"Melissa, this is WITSEC Inspector Deputy Marshal Miles Ackerman. He's going to be taking point on yours and Dylan's protection." Miles was too well-trained to even blink when Griffin used his false name. Ackerman was the name he gave witnesses to hide his true identity. It was just one of the security measures they went through in order to keep his personal life private. "Miles, this is Melissa Morgan."

She started to reach for his hand, but the child in her arms slipped through her grip and ran to jump on the bed. She hurried after him, pulling him off and trying to settle him down. "I'm sorry about that," she told Miles. "It's nice to meet you."

"You, too," Miles responded.

"Melissa was only five years old when her mother entered WITSEC," Griffin explained. "Her mother never told her. She had no idea she was raised in the program until the marshals showed up at the police station after her mother's death."

He felt for her having to learn the truth that way, but that was the nature of WITSEC, hiding the truth from everyone you loved.

"I'm sorry for your loss," Miles told her.

She gripped her son tighter and bit her lip. "Thank you."

Griffin turned back to Melissa. "Sorry, I know it's difficult. But Miles is one of our top WITSEC inspectors. He'll take good care of both you and Dylan." Griffin turned his focus to Miles. "I went ahead and dismissed the previous marshals, the ones who transported Melissa and Dylan here. That way, no one can tie you to her protection detail. That also means you'll be on your own once I leave."

Miles nodded. "I understand."

"You have my number if you need to reach me." He said goodbye to Melissa, then walked out.

Miles surveyed the room. First things first. He needed to make certain they were secure. He went to the door and locked it, then checked the windows.

Melissa watched him then shook her head. "The other guy already did that. And the guy before him."

"I'm sure they did, but I like to make sure of things myself."

She stood. "So far, I've had six marshals watching over me and every one of them did the same thing. Is that something you learn in training—not to trust each other?"

He shrugged. "It's not a question of trust. Just good security measures."

She fidgeted with her fingers. "Well, they didn't turn out to be so good, did they?"

He saw the fear and frustration in her face and wanted to say something to reassure her. "You're still alive, aren't you, ma'am?"

"We were nearly killed several times."

"You know what they say, don't you? '*Nearly* only counts in horseshoes and hand grenades.'"

He spotted the little boy now clinging to his mother's leg, his eyes wide with fright. All his energy seemed to have evaporated in an instant. Miles kneeled and addressed him. "Hello there. My name is Miles. What's yours?"

The boy dug his face into Melissa's leg rather than reply.

Melissa gave a half-hearted smile. "He's not usually shy, but these past weeks have been hard on him. So many new people in and out."

"I understand."

"His name is Dylan. He's three." She shuddered again. "Nearly the same age I was when my mother entered the program. How could she not tell me?"

He stood and turned his attention to her. "I'm sure she was just trying to protect you. By the time you were old enough to understand, a lot of time had passed since the trial. She thought she was safe."

Melissa sat down and handed Dylan a toy giraffe to play with. "She was always so cautious. I used to tease her about how uptight she was. Now, I understand why she was like that. I just wish she had told me. My entire life has been a lie."

"Your mom loved you—that's always been true," he said gently. "From what I just read in her file, she gave up everything to protect you, to keep you safe." He glanced at Dylan, who had started bouncing on the bed with the toy giraffe. "He's an active little boy, isn't he?"

"He is. He's hardly ever still except when he's sleeping. It's tough for him to be cooped up in hotel rooms for weeks—away from all of his things, not allowed to go outside and play. It's hard on both of us."

He reached for her hand, intending only to reassure her that things were going to be okay, but the way her petite hand felt in his sent him reeling. He tried to push down the feeling. Yes, this woman was innocent and she and her son didn't deserve what was happening to them. But he had to remind himself that life wasn't fair. If it was, he would be out of a job. It was only natural that he feel some sympathy for them, but he couldn't let that cloud his judgment. They needed him to stay sharp.

"Let's just get through this one day at a time, okay?" She nodded and turned her attention back to Dylan.

Miles walked to the window and tried to regain his own composure. It wasn't his job to get close to his witnesses, but he'd found offering a sympathetic ear helped them to cope with the abrupt changes happening in their lives. It also built trust between them. But he had to be careful with this one. He'd protected mothers before, even single mothers and their children, but something about this pretty, young woman and her child was tugging at his heartstrings like no one ever had before. He suspected it had more to do with his recent breakup than with his witness. He'd come home from helping to care for his dad only to discover his girlfriend had left him. Even though his absence hadn't been connected to work at all, she'd decided she couldn't build a relationship with a man whose frequent absences made him incapable of sharing his life with her.

It wasn't the first time his job had gotten in the way of his love life, and he doubted it would be the last. But he couldn't regret his commitment to his work. Not when there were people like this woman and child, who deserved all the help and protection they could get.

He was ready to settle down and start a family, but it seemed that particular dream wasn't going to happen for him anytime soon…if at all.

He rechecked the room to make sure everything was secure. It gave him something to do besides sit and wait, but it failed to keep his mind busy. He was still thinking about Dylan and how difficult it was going to be to keep an energetic little boy from running off and attracting attention. They needed someplace safe, where they could go so Dylan could run and jump, a safe house with a large living room perhaps or... No, he couldn't go there. He'd never taken anyone back to his family's ranch and he couldn't see himself starting now. He wasn't going to ask his family to put themselves at risk.

A knock on the door grabbed his attention and his hand instantly went to his gun. Melissa grabbed Dylan and pulled him to her as Miles walked to the door.

"Who is it?" he asked.

A voice replied, "Room service. We have your dinner, sir."

Miles frowned. He hadn't ordered anything, but he supposed it was possible Griffin had placed an order. He'd let the waiter in...but he'd stay on his guard.

He unlocked the door and opened it, positioning himself behind the door with his hand on his gun just in case as a waiter pushed a cart inside with several trays on top. The man flashed Melissa and Dylan a smile then turned to Miles, handing him the receipt to sign.

Once Miles took it, the waiter then reached under the cart, pushed aside the tablecloth and grabbed hold of something.

He was going for a gun.

Miles dropped the receipt book and pulled his weapon. "Don't move!" he shouted as the man spun around. Miles kicked him, sending him sprawling backward over the cart and to the floor on the other side of the bed. He raised his gun and shouted for Melissa to grab Dylan and run.

Without hesitating, she swooped up the child and took off down the hallway toward the elevators. Miles backed from the room, keeping one eye on her and the other on the attacker. When he poked his head up, Miles fired and the man ducked for cover again. Miles heard the elevator door ding, indicating it was there, and he didn't wait around to see if he'd hit the attacker. He took off running, dashing into the elevator just before the doors slid closed. He hit the button to the basement and willed the elevator to move quickly.

Melissa tried to comfort Dylan, who was frightened and crying. Miles quelled a desire to tell her to quiet him. He knew how difficult that would be. Still, a crying child was a dead giveaway to their location. He could only hope Dylan would calm down on his own before the elevator doors opened again.

They had to get out of here now. If Shearer's men had infiltrated the hotel, there might be more than one attacker coming after her.

The elevator reached the basement and Miles braced himself for a fight. He raised his gun, ready to fire if anyone was waiting for them. The doors opened and he breathed a sigh of relief that no one was there. Either the shooter was working alone, or his backup was staking out the lobby or some other exit. Still, Miles wouldn't let down his guard. They needed to get out of this hotel before he came after them.

He hustled Melissa and Dylan toward his SUV and hurried them inside, glad to see that Griffin had had the forethought to install Dylan's car seat before he'd left. Melissa crawled into the back seat with Dylan as Miles slid behind the wheel.

"Put your head down until I tell you it's clear," he ordered as he sped out of his parking space and toward the exit.

Their attacker emerged at the exit ramp. He raised a gun at them, but Miles wasn't going to be deterred. He hit the accelerator and sped toward the man. The guy fired several shots that hit the windshield but the bullet-resistant glass didn't break.

He rammed the accelerator and aimed the car right for the exit. If this guy wanted to get out of his way, fine. If not, he was going to get hit.

The guy jumped out of the path of the car just in time as Miles turned out of the garage and headed for the interstate.

"Are you both okay?" he asked as he merged into traffic and checked his mirrors to see the attacker running after them on foot. He wouldn't catch up to them, but Miles kept an eye on him, anyway, to make sure he didn't enter a vehicle of his own and give chase.

"We're okay," Melissa told him, but her voice sounded shaky with fear. That was to be expected.

"Stay low for now." He pulled his phone from his pocket and dialed his boss's number. "Griffin, they found us at the hotel."

"What? Already? How?"

"I don't know, but there was an attacker. He came in, pretending to be bringing room service. Get down to the hotel and see what you can find out. I'm taking them to a safer place. I'll let you know when we land somewhere."

He ended the call. He didn't tell Griffin where he was going. He didn't know himself yet. There were two other backup safe houses. One of them was only six blocks away, but when he checked his mirrors and spotted a car that looked suspicious, he questioned going there just yet. He made a left turn and the car followed him, so he tried more evasive measures. The car kept on their tail.

They were definitely being followed.

It seemed the attacker had an accomplice after all.

He hit the redial button on his phone. "I have a black SUV following us. I'm nixing the West Street safe house."

"I'll call the local cops and have the car stopped. Where are you?"

"Eighth and Main Avenue, turning right onto Riverside."

"I've got cars headed to your location now."

He turned and again the SUV kept up. He glanced into the back seat. Melissa was crouched on the floorboards, her body tucked around her son's and her eyes wide with fear. He had to keep them safe. Dylan was still crying, but she was doing her best to comfort him and keep him quiet. At this point, it wouldn't put them in any more danger whether he screamed or not, but it sure would help Miles's concentration if he was quiet.

He turned again and screeched to a stop. Traffic was bumper-to-bumper. He grimaced. This wasn't good. The black SUV pulled up behind him. He drove aggressively and managed to move up two spaces in the other lane, but they weren't going forward anytime soon and the SUV had blocked their way backward.

Miles rammed the vehicle into Park and reached for his phone and his gun. "We have to move now." He crawled across the front seat to the passenger side and pushed open the door. He raised his gun, then opened the back door for Melissa and Dylan. She emerged carrying the boy in her arms and he pushed her forward, through the mass of motionless cars, positioning his body between her and the SUV.

The men in the SUV saw them and got out, revealing their own weapons.

"Run," Miles shouted as he raised his gun and fired, hitting the black SUV. The two men began returning fire and Miles turned and ran after Melissa.

People in their cars began to scream and jump out of their vehicles at the sound of gunfire, trying to get to safety. Miles stopped every few feet and fired off a few rounds, shooting high to keep from hitting anyone. He didn't like putting innocent bystanders in danger, but he couldn't do anything to stop the bad guys from firing their weapons into the crowd. Nothing except giving up, which he wasn't prepared to do. The chaos was good for them, though. It helped give Melissa and Dylan cover as they ran. And he was sure to keep up with them.

He heard sirens, and moments later several police cars appeared. The men went in opposite directions, but stopped pursuing them. Miles saw one disappear into a store and the other into an alleyway. The police called for Miles to stop, too, but he didn't. He couldn't lose Melissa in the crowd. He had to remain with her. He turned and took off running, hoping the cops wouldn't fire in a crowd of people like the bad guys had.

They didn't, and soon their shouts to stop were nothing more than voices on the wind. Catching up with Melissa and Dylan, he pushed them into a crowded restaurant, through the kitchen and out the back door into an alleyway, ignoring the protests of the restaurant staff. He took out his phone and called Griffin again.

"Any news?"

"The shooters got away, but the local police department has their car. Maybe we can get some answers from that."

He doubted it. It was probably stolen or had been rented under a false identification, and the men were almost certainly wearing gloves to avoid leaving fingerprints. These guys weren't amateurs.

"Where are you?" Griffin asked.

"Still on the street, but I haven't seen any signs of the shooters. They scattered after the cops arrived." He ended the call, then motioned for Melissa to crouch behind the dumpster in the alley. "Let me check out the street."

She nodded and ducked down, pulling Dylan with her.

He walked to the end of the alleyway. People were milling around, coming and going, oblivious to the commotion they'd caused, which had been several blocks away. He didn't see any sign of the shooters or anyone who appeared to be looking for them. He spotted a cab turning from the opposite direction and silently sighed in relief. He walked into the street and hailed it, leaning into the driver's window to check his identification against the driver's face before he motioned for Melissa and Dylan to come out.

She hurried from the alley and climbed into the cab, seating Dylan on her lap. Miles slid in beside them and told the driver to head to the airport. The driver turned the cab around and headed back in the opposite direction.

"Are we taking a flight?" she asked Miles.

He shook his head but lowered his voice. "We'll rent a car at the airport."

Once the cab dropped them off, he headed toward the car-rental desk.

"I also need to rent a car seat," he told the clerk. Dylan's car seat was back in his SUV and they were not going back that way.

His mind was already ticking as he tried to figure out how Shearer's men had found her at the hotel. Griffin had made those arrangements and Miles had double-checked everything to make certain they were secure. She should have been safe. Unless…

The clerk handed over the keys, along with the car seat, and Miles led Melissa and Dylan toward the vehicle, keeping a hand on her back and his eyes on a constant scan, making sure no one was watching them. He helped install the car seat and stood guard as Melissa buckled Dylan in, then crawled in beside him. Miles slid into the driver's seat of the rented SUV, but before he started the engine, he turned to Melissa. He needed to see her face as he asked these questions. "Have you made any calls? Phoned anyone? A friend, a relative, Dylan's day care?"

She shook her head. "No one. Why?"

"I'm just trying to figure out how they found us at the hotel."

Her brow creased and anger lit her eyes. "I didn't call anyone. I haven't broken any of the rules. Those other marshals tried to accuse me of making a mistake, too, but I wouldn't do anything to put my son in danger. Trust me, I know the risks."

He believed her. She'd witnessed her mother's murder. She knew the risks all too well. But that didn't explain how yet another safe house had been compromised, especially when such precautions had been taken. He didn't like what that indicated. No witness assigned to his office's detail who'd followed the rules had ever been killed, and he wasn't ready to change that statistic. He was proud of it. But he was baffled by her case and understood why Griffin wanted this protection detail kept quiet from the rest of the office.

He hated even considering it, but he couldn't ignore the facts. If Melissa had followed the rules—and he believed she had—then the only ones who could have known her location were the agents who had guarded her before Miles arrived.

And that meant Griffin was right—someone in WITSEC *was* a mole.

TWO

He drove for five hours before pulling in at a motel and paying for a room. Dylan and Melissa had both fallen asleep during the drive. The stress on her face was enough to tell him she needed the sleep and he considered driving on. But he was tired, dead tired, and he needed a break, too, if not to sleep then to just rest while he processed all that had happened.

He understood the danger Griffin had warned him about. Whoever was after this woman and her son was fearless and had access to information that was supposed to be secret. He didn't like believing there was a mole in WITSEC, but how else could he account for the multiple breaches of safe houses? He couldn't.

He considered their options. He had an official credit card he used to pay for anything witnesses needed during their initial relocation, but any charges could be traced by someone in the agency. Using it would give away his location *and* it would indicate that he was the one who was on Melissa's case, since, officially, he was supposed to be away from work and shouldn't have needed the card at all.

He could turn to a friend for help, but Griffin wanted him to do this on his own and now he understood why. Even the phones at the US Marshals Service could be compromised. He had no idea how deep the mole's interference went, and he couldn't risk her life that way.

Which meant he was operating with no backup and no resources except for what he had on him, which amounted to his gun, his phone and—he checked his wallet—a hundred and twelve dollars in cash. Good thing he'd made that ATM stop before meeting Griffin at the hotel.

They needed somewhere to go where they could be out of the public eye. Whoever was after Melissa had the weight of the marshals information service at their disposal, which meant the most modern technology, including facial-recognition software and access to police status updates. No, being out in the open on their own was too dangerous. But any safe house known to the marshals service wasn't feasible.

He saw only one option and it was one he didn't like, but it would certainly solve their problems. If he couldn't count on his colleagues to have his back, the only other people he trusted in the world were his brothers.

Griffin had said he was telling people that Miles was returning to his family's home. No one would have any reason to think he was connected to the case, so no one would be monitoring his family. Shearer had no reason to look for her at the ranch, which meant the twenty-six-acre spread would be an ideal place to keep Melissa safe. It would even allow Dylan a little running room. And with his brothers and sister around, he would have backup if things went sideways.

Tomorrow morning, he would pick up a burner cell phone at a convenience store and phone his brother Josh, the current sheriff of Courtland County, Texas— the county that held his family's ranch. But he needed a way to explain Melissa and Dylan's presence that didn't raise any red flags to anyone in town.

He sighed and realized his family was in for a shock when they arrived.

Melissa jerked up in bed, suddenly realizing that she'd dozed off. The room was quiet and Dylan was still sleeping beside her. Miles was up, sitting at the table and working on something.

"It's okay," he said softly. "It's still nighttime. You've only been asleep for three hours."

She sat up on the bed and rubbed her eyes, surprised she'd even dozed off. She hadn't wanted to let her guard down even though she was so tired. The marshals service wasn't impressing her with their ability to keep her and her son safe.

But something about Miles's quiet strength did reassure her. As did his broad shoulders and deep green eyes.

She shook off those thoughts. Where had they come from, anyway? She hadn't noticed a man since her husband had passed, and she was certain it was only Miles's close proximity and the fact that she was sleep-deprived and half out of her mind with fear that was making her think such things. He had saved them from a dangerous situation and she was grateful. Nothing more.

She stood and stretched out her arms and legs, then walked over to the table to see what he was doing. He'd cut up the documents the other marshal had given her and it looked like he was making up new ones. She sighed. "Time to change identities again?"

He nodded. "I've decided to take you someplace where I know you'll be safe."

"Where's that?"

He hesitated and she understood. She'd been through this too many times in the past weeks. "Oh, yeah. You're not supposed to tell me until we get there, right?"

"Right."

"Where did you get the supplies to do this?"

"Borrowed what I needed from the front desk." He handed her new identification to her.

The photo was the same one she'd had on her original driver's license, but the last name was different and it showed a Dallas address. "Melissa Avery. So I take it we're going to Dallas?"

He shook his head and cleaned up. "No, we're not, but we're going close enough that a Dallas ID won't stand out as unusual."

He cleaned up his clippings and she glanced at another document, this one hidden beneath a notebook with only the corner sticking out. She pulled it out and saw the words *Certificate of Marriage* with both hers and Miles's first names but different last names for each of them.

"What's this?"

"We're going deep undercover. The best way for me to protect you is to be with you twenty-four-seven and the best way to do that is to pretend to be your husband."

She nodded. It made sense. Whoever was after her was looking for a single mom and child, not a family. "Okay."

He gave her a look of surprise. "You don't object?"

It was obvious that he'd expected her to argue, but she was too weary for that. And too determined. At this point, she would do whatever it took to keep her child safe. "Why should I? After what we've been through and what I've seen, I'll do whatever's necessary to protect Dylan. If that means pretending to be your wife, then I'll be your wife. It's not like you're asking me to really marry you, right?" She chuckled and looked at him. She saw something flash in his expression before he concealed it.

"No, I'm afraid I wouldn't make good husband material."

She wondered why he would say that. He seemed like a kind and decent man, and so far, he'd been nothing but protective of them. That may have been his job, but it was the job of anyone who chose to be a marshal—and he'd definitely treated them better than the last three marshals who had been assigned to her case.

"I guess I'll have to tell Dylan to start calling you Daddy." She sighed as she looked at her son. "This entire experience is going to do a number on him, isn't it? I just hope it doesn't scar him for life."

"Once you get somewhere settled, he won't even remember this, more than likely."

"How could he ever forget something like this? The running, and changing names?"

"You did—and you were already a few years older than Dylan."

She hadn't even thought of that. The only reason her mother had been able to keep this gigantic secret from her was because Melissa had no memory of it. "I guess I did."

"Kids are resilient that way. He's fortunate to have a mother who loves him so much." She stared at her son and tears filled her eyes. She wanted so much for him, so much more than a life on the run.

"Can I ask what happened to his father?"

"You mean it's not written down in my file?"

"No, it is, but I'd like to hear it from you."

She pushed away a stray tear that had gotten loose. "His name was Vick. We were high-school sweethearts, married right after graduation. He was driving home from work one evening and was hit by a drunk driver. The police said he died on impact." She glanced at her son. "Dylan was only four months old. If I hadn't had my mom there to help me, I don't know how I would have handled it." A swell of grief filled her as she thought about her mother and the terrible way she'd died. She wanted her mother with her now to help their family work through this. She reached into her pocket and fingered the chain of her mother's necklace. It helped soothe her having that tiny bit of her mom with her.

"I'm sorry for your loss." His words were quiet and kind, and she nodded, thanking him as several more tears slipped from her eyes. "We'll stick as close to the truth about his death as possible, but if anyone asks about him, try to avoid many details. Just say he died in a car wreck."

She understood his reasoning but the details were what made Vick's death real to her. Miles was taking away Vick's identity by denying them.

"I know it's hard, but the more details you give, the easier it is for someone to be able to look Vick up and figure out his identity—and then connect that back to you."

"Why bring him up at all? If we're going to pretend to be married, why can't we pretend Dylan is your child?"

He grimaced then shook his head. "That's not going to work where we're going. You'll understand once we get there." He stood and picked up his gun holster, clipping it to his belt. "I'm going to do a sweep of the area. I'll be back in a few minutes."

She locked the door behind him, suspecting he was doing this only to give her the space she needed to grieve. She appreciated that gesture.

She picked up the marriage license with her name on it and stared at it, looking specifically at Miles's name. She'd only had one marriage license in her life and it had been with Vick. That had been a special bond, a dream of hers since tenth grade. This was a necessity and she hated every minute of it.

But she was determined to get herself and her son through this experience. And if that meant becoming Mrs. Miles Avery, then so be it.

Miles was quiet as they drove for hours the next day. She wasn't familiar with the area, so she had no idea where they were going or how much longer it would take to get there, and she knew better than to ask. But she was ready to be out of this car and so was Dylan. He'd gotten whiny and restless as the hours rolled on. Thankfully, a toy from a fast-food restaurant where they'd stopped for an early lunch had calmed him for a bit, but she knew it wouldn't be long before he was restless once again.

Eventually, Miles pulled the car to the side of the road and cut the engine. Melissa saw no buildings in sight, only open land and fields for as far as she could see.

"Why are we stopping?"

He pulled out the wedding ring he'd purchased from a pawn shop an hour ago and handed it to her. "You should probably put this on."

She glanced at it then nodded and slipped the ring onto her finger. "I nearly forgot. We're supposed to be married."

"There's something else you should know before we arrive. This place where we're going is my family's ranch. I know you'll be safe there. No one has any reason to suspect you'd be here, and if anyone does come for you, my brothers will be there to help me protect you and I trust them with my life."

She liked the idea of a ranch, a place where Dylan could get outside and have some fresh air instead of being cooped up inside a motel room. "Okay, but then why the name change? Won't your family find it strange that you're using an assumed name?"

"That's the other thing. Ackerman is the name I use for witnesses to protect my real identity. Miles Avery is my real name."

"I see." She didn't know how to process that but she supposed it made sense that even the marshals had false identities.

"There's something else. My family knows I work for the marshals service, but they don't know about the WITSEC part. They think I protect judges and track down fugitives for a living."

She sighed and leaned back in her seat. She saw what he was hinting at. "You have a lot of secrets, don't you?"

"Secrecy has to be a part of my job. It protects everyone."

"So what did you tell your family about me and Dylan?"

"Nothing yet, but the story will be that I met a woman who had a child and we got married last week."

"So you want me to lie to your family?"

"Telling them the truth would just put them in danger. I'm taking a huge risk by bringing you here, Melissa. I truly believe this is the safest place for both you and Dylan. But my job and my ability to keep you safe depend on secrecy. Can you do that?"

She didn't understand how he could keep a secret like that from his family, but that wasn't her business. She had her own family to think about—her and Dylan. If playing a charade with people she didn't know was the best option, then that was what she'd do. And after all, wasn't that what her life would be from now on, anyway? One big charade? Even if she hadn't realized it, wasn't that what her life had been all along?

She nodded her agreement and he restarted the car and drove a little bit farther, turning onto a dirt road and through an entrance that read Silver Star Ranch. He steered down the long driveway and stopped the car in front of a white farmhouse with a wraparound porch. She noticed a barn and horses on one side and a garden on the other.

"Mama, look! Horses!" Dylan shouted with glee, causing both her and Miles to laugh at the excitement in his voice.

"That's right, buddy. We've got horses," Miles said. He got out and walked around the car to unbuckle Dylan as Melissa unfastened her seat belt and got out.

The front door of the house opened and a group of people emerged.

Miles took her hand then leaned in and whispered to her, "Remember to breathe," before pulling her toward the crowd.

She spotted the looks of surprise on their faces and calmed herself by counting. There was an older couple, probably his parents, three men around Miles's age and two women approximately her age.

"Hey, Mama. Hey, Daddy." His parents walked over

to greet them. He gave his mother a quick hug and a kiss on the cheek, then shook his father's hand before turning to Melissa. "Melissa, this is my mom and dad, John and Diane Avery." He pointed at the others on the porch. "These are my brothers, Josh, Paul and Lawson, as well as Lawson's wife, Bree, and my sister, Kellyanne. I have another brother, Colby, who isn't here. Everyone, I'd like you all to meet Melissa and her son, Dylan."

"How do you do," she said, addressing them, and they all nodded and returned her greeting.

He slid his hand into hers and a shiver of electricity snaked up her arm as he pulled her closer to him. "Melissa is…my wife."

He'd expected an uproar when he dropped his bombshell, but he hadn't been prepared for the one that occurred. Hurt riddled his family's eyes as they descended on him.

"What do you mean *wife*?" his sister demanded, stomping down the porch steps and toward him until she was right in his face. "You got married? Without inviting any of us? How could you do that, Miles?"

The rest of the family echoed her comments, making him glad they lived out in the country, where the neighbors couldn't hear such an uproar. He didn't like seeing the anger and sadness in their faces, but he reminded himself that this deception was necessary to keep Melissa safe. Still, he could see Melissa was horrified and moved closer to him.

His father took charge and stepped forward, pulling away Kellyanne. "Stop it, stop it, all of you. You'll make this young lady believe we're a family of nay-sayers." He reached for Miles's hand to shake it again. "Congratulations, son." Then he pulled Melissa into a hug. "Welcome to the family."

"Thank you," she said.

His mother followed suit and gave them each a big hug. "Yes, congratulations. Forgive us for not saying that right away. This is just such a shock. Miles never tells us anything. Getting any information out of him is like getting water from a stone." She turned to Dylan, who was still in Miles's arms and looking a little skittish as he clung to Miles's neck. "And who is this?"

"This is Dylan. He's Melissa's son from her first marriage. Her husband was killed in a car accident two years ago."

"Hello, Dylan." Her eyes lit up at the prospect of having a little one around and Miles hated the deception all over again because he knew they'd have to tell them the truth at some point. His mom would be devastated to learn that he'd deceived her, especially when their cover story gave her a grandson she wouldn't be able to keep. But she would eventually understand. Besides, this might be her only opportunity to enjoy the pleasure of having a grandchild, at least where he was concerned. His brothers and sister may one day give her all the grandkids she longed for, but he doubted he ever would. His last girlfriend's words to him reverberated in his mind. He would never have a normal family life with kids and a wife because his life would never be normal. His job required secrets and what kind of a relationship could he ever build with the secrets he hid?

He carried Dylan inside and could tell the boy was overwhelmed by his family.

"Why don't I take Dylan into the kitchen?" his mother suggested. "I just made a fresh batch of chocolate-chip cookies. Would you like one, Dylan?"

He nodded and took her hand as she led him into the next room. He saw the concern on Melissa's face at having her son out of her sight, but he pulled her to him, to reassure her. "He'll be fine. He's just right there."

She nodded and accepted it, but her eyes kept flitting toward the kitchen. He was impressed at how strong she was. She met every challenge better than most of the witnesses he worked with. He'd seen people in a lot less danger fall apart at the thought of change, but she was rising to the occasion impressively.

"So where did you and Miles meet?" Kellyanne asked, sidling up to Melissa and crooking an arm through hers.

Thankfully, they'd gone through a cover story, but Miles still listened close to see if she stayed on script.

"A friend of a friend introduced us. She said Miles was a great guy." She turned and smiled at him. "Obviously, she was right."

After the obligatory get-to-know-you phase with his family, he pulled her aside then went after Dylan, who had already taken a shine to his mom.

"Josh said we could stay at his cabin. It's a quarter mile down the road, but we'll still be on the property."

"You're not staying at the main house?" his mother asked, her voice full of hurt.

"They need their privacy," his father stated. "Go ahead, Miles, but be sure to come back here for supper with the family."

He nodded and ushered Dylan and Melissa back outside to the car. He then buckled Dylan into his car seat as Melissa settled herself up front. Once he'd started the car, turned around and headed toward the cabin, she slumped over. "I hate lying to your family. They seem like nice people."

"They are nice."

"You don't trust them then to keep the secret?"

"I trust every one of them with my life."

"Then why all the lies?"

"It has to be that way, Melissa. Don't you see? Being honest with them about what I do would only place them in danger. As long as they don't know about WITSEC, they won't ask questions about what I'm doing or worry about the risks I face."

"I'm sure your mom worries about you no matter what."

"Yeah, well, trying to stop my mom from worrying is like fighting a bull."

She glanced into the back seat and gave a small smile, and he could see worrying about your children was something she could relate to. "I guess you're right."

He sighed and opened up to her. "There are other factors involved, too. Not every witness I relocate is an innocent victim like yourself. In fact, most of them are criminals, testifying against their bosses in exchange for leniency. If they knew my real identity or about my family, they could use that info as leverage against me."

"Then why do you do it? Why take so many risks to protect people like that?"

He gave her a small shrug and tried to sound nonchalant. "It's what I do." But when he saw the disbelief in her face, he decided to be honest with her. He parked the truck in front of Josh's cabin and put it in Park, but didn't get out. "When I was fourteen, there was this gang that took up residence in town. My dad was sheriff back then and I spent a lot of time at the sheriff's office. One day, a call came in about an old man, a rancher named Robert Bullock. He was eighty years old and he'd been found beaten nearly to death. He'd had a run-in with the gang the day before and they'd bragged about beating him up and taking his truck. My dad tried to arrest those men, only no one who heard them bragging about it would come forward to testify against them."

"How awful."

"People were scared. I remember the fear everyone felt. I also remember how frustrated my dad was at the whole town. He was trying to put away bad guys, violent men, only everyone involved was too scared to help him. It only would have taken one person stepping up, and the whole town would have been safer—but no one was willing to take that risk. When I joined the marshals service, I knew I wanted to see people brought to justice, people like those men, and sometimes that means making a deal. It's my job to protect those people who risk their lives to come forward so that we can put away the really bad guys."

He turned to look at her and saw tears pooling in her eyes. "People like my mom."

He reached out to touch her arm, sending a spark of electricity between them. The cab of the truck filled with tension and he saw in her face that she felt it, too. He broke their connection by opening the door and getting out. As he walked around the car, he took a deep breath to calm his racing pulse. His attraction to this woman would do nothing but put her life in danger. It was clear that nothing could ever happen between them. She hated secrets, and keeping secrets was his way of life.

She took Dylan's hand and they walked into Josh's cabin. He'd built it intending to marry his high-school girlfriend right out of college, which he'd done, but their marriage had lasted barely two months before she'd been murdered in this very cabin. Afterward, Josh had poured himself into his work at the sheriff's office, eventually winning election as sheriff once their dad retired.

Miles opened the door to the spare bedroom. "You and Dylan can stay in here. I'll take the other room."

She glanced around, then turned back to him. "Are you sure we're safe here?"

"Absolutely. No one knows you're here. Even my office doesn't know we've come here and, I promise, my brothers are the best backup we could ask for."

He left her and Dylan alone to settle in. He understood this was a lot for her to take in all at once. She and her son had been through so much over the past weeks and they deserved a reprieve. He hoped being here on the Silver Star could provide them with that. This land had been his home and place of retreat for as long as he could remember. When nothing else was going right in his life, his heart always returned here to the Silver Star—to the vast fields and open sky where every star was visible and you could get lost on the horizon.

Maybe tomorrow he would take them both on a horseback ride to see the full spread. It would do Dylan some good to be able to get out and stretch his legs and run, and it would also do Melissa good to be outside in the sunshine and fresh air.

Of course, they would have to go into town to get some clothes first. He might be able to borrow something from Kellyanne or Bree for her, but with no other children on the ranch, finding something for Dylan would be more difficult. Plus, he was sure they were ready for some fresh provisions since they'd been living out of a hastily packed bag for weeks, bags that had been left behind when they'd fled from the hotel.

He couldn't use his marshals-service credit card, but no one would blink at him using his personal credit cards in his own hometown—and that was if they were going through his financials, which he doubted anyone would.

He would let them rest for an hour or so, then they would head into town. He'd introduced her to the family. Now, it was time to introduce her to Courtland County.

THREE

Melissa was excited at first when Miles suggested they go into town to do some shopping, but as they got back into his SUV and headed off the ranch, panic filled her.

"Are you sure this is safe?" she asked.

The other marshals had gone to such lengths to make sure she didn't see or talk to anyone and here was Miles parading her around town.

"We'll be fine," he told her. "No one in Courtland is looking for you. As far as anyone is concerned, you're my wife. It would be more suspicious if I hid you away."

"What about video cameras? Won't the store have those? Street cameras? If there's a leak in the marshals office, won't they have access to those feeds?"

He flashed her an incredulous look at her mention of the leak. She wasn't supposed to know about that.

"I could tell the breaches in my security weren't usual, and I saw your boss's concern. It doesn't take a genius to figure out there must be a leak in your office."

"I trust my fellow marshals with my life, but you

are right. This is an unusual situation. You don't need to worry. I'll keep you and Dylan safe while Griffin searches for the leak." He gave a small chuckle and grinned at her. "And to your question about the cameras, this is Courtland County. We're a little behind the times down here. There are no street cameras and the security feeds at any store or restaurant in town won't be sophisticated enough for effective facial recognition." He reached across the seat and squeezed her hand. "Trust me, Melissa. I know this town like the back of my hand. You're safe here."

She leaned back in her seat and tried to calm down. She wanted to believe him, and she liked that he hadn't tried to hide the issue with someone in his office giving away her locations. With all the lying they were doing, his honesty was refreshing. So far, she liked being here. She liked Miles's family, too. She'd never had a big family with lots of brothers and sisters or aunts and uncles, but she'd always secretly wanted it, even if she'd never said anything, not wanting to make her mother feel bad. It had always just been her and her mom. Even when she'd married Vick, he'd been an only child whose parents had died when he was twelve. After that, he'd been raised in group homes until he aged out of foster care. She enjoyed being surrounded by people who seemed to care about one another, and she didn't quite understand how Miles could keep them at a distance the way he did. Sure, she understood about the importance of his job and the need for secrecy, but did he not understand how blessed he was to come from such a large, loving family?

He pulled up in front of a building with a sign that read Miss Robbie's General Store. She got out while Miles took Dylan from his car seat and held his hand as they walked inside. She liked the way this full-grown man looked beside her little boy. But even better than the visual was the attention he paid to Dylan. It warmed her heart and told her everything she might ever need to know about Miles Avery. He was a good man with a good heart, and she was thankful he'd been the one assigned to protect them.

Together, Miles and Dylan held open the door for her. "Ladies first," Miles said then Dylan parroted his words in his three-year-old pronunciation.

"Wadies furst."

She bent and kissed Dylan's nose before walking inside.

They were greeted by a pretty woman with dark hair and a big smile. "Miles, hi!" She walked around the counter and gave him a hug, which he returned stiffly.

"Hi, Ellie." He turned to Melissa. "Ellie Mansfield, this is Melissa Avery."

Ellie gave her a confused look. "Avery?"

"My wife."

Ellie frowned a bit as that information sank in, but then she smiled and pulled Miles in for another hug. "Well, congratulations, you two." She turned to Melissa. "I can't believe Miles finally settled down. You know, we used to date when we were in high school."

He looked uncomfortable, then interjected, "Yes, well, that was a long time ago."

"Yes, it was."

"I didn't know you were back in town. Last I'd heard, you got married and moved away."

She grimaced. "Your information is out of date. We're divorced. I stayed with my aunt in Dallas for a while then moved back to town a few weeks ago."

"Oh, I'm sorry to hear about the divorce."

She shrugged. "I guess that's life. Now, what can I help you two find today?"

"We're just here to do some shopping. I think we can find what we need on our own." He glanced at Melissa. "Right?"

"Right."

As Ellie returned to the counter, Melissa checked out the store. It was a hodgepodge of merchandise ranging from clothing to groceries to farm accessories. At the far end was a small diner with a counter and tables and chairs. Miles led them toward the clothing and instructed her to pick out whatever she needed.

"How are we going to pay for this?" The marshals had taken her credit and bank cards from her and although they'd promised her funds would eventually come through once they'd been scrubbed through their system and deposited under her new identity, she still didn't have access to them.

"I've got it taken care of," he insisted. "Whatever you need."

"I can't let you spend your own money on me," she told him and he shushed her by placing his finger over her lips, then leaned in to whisper to her.

"Why wouldn't I spend my own money on my wife? It would look odd if I didn't, wouldn't it?"

She conceded, though she was silently intent on repaying him once her money came through. She picked out two pairs of jeans and two tops, along with some other necessities, then caught up with Miles, who had Dylan sitting on the checkout counter along with several tiny cowboy outfits, a pair of kids' boots and a cowboy hat.

Despite how cute he looked in the cowboy hat, she quickly protested. "He doesn't need all this stuff."

"He doesn't *not* need it, either. I'm just having a little fun. Besides, he loves it, don't you, buddy?"

Dylan lit up with a smile and nodded. "Don't I look pretty, Mama?"

Despite the pang of guilt at how much this was costing Miles, she couldn't resist, realizing how much her little boy had been through in the past weeks. If a new hat made him happy, she wasn't going to disappoint him. "Thank you," she whispered, sidling up beside Miles.

"You're welcome." He turned to the woman at the checkout. "Ellie, would you ring us up? Then I think we're going to grab a burger while we're here."

He slung Dylan over his shoulder as the boy giggled and waved to her. She waved back and watched them. This was the most fun her baby boy had had in weeks and she was thankful for this man who'd come into their lives and saw them as more than just a job.

"He's a cutie," Ellie told her as she leaned across the counter.

"Thank you."

"And Miles is so good with him. He's going to make a great daddy to your little boy."

Melissa stood and stared at her, shock making her unable to speak. She knew Ellie was just responding to what she'd been told about their relationship, but her words made Melissa realize for the first time just how taken Dylan had become with the handsome US Marshal. She had to watch out that they didn't become too close to him, because the connection couldn't last. Once the men after her were captured, they would be moving on to a new location and a new life. No matter how attentive he was, or how safe she felt with him, she had to remember that Miles was only doing his job—and before long, that job would end. He wasn't in their lives to stay.

She joined the guys for burgers and fries at the diner. She had so many other things to worry about than her son getting too attached, but now she had yet another thing to face once this was all over. How to explain the situation to Dylan once Miles disappeared from their lives.

They had supper at the main house with the family, giving Melissa a chance to get to know everyone better. Melissa and Kellyanne seemed to click right away and his kid sister took up immediately with Dylan, fawning over the boy.

He was glad to see the Christmas decorations were up inside the house and the tree in the corner was lit. It hadn't been earlier, but now that it was dark outside, Dylan was fascinated by the twinkling of the lights on the tree. Miles knew from experience that once all the trimmings were in place, this tree would look stunning.

Miles took an opportunity when everyone was focused on Melissa, and not him, to slip out onto the porch. He phoned Griffin to get an update on the investigation into the leak at the WITSEC office.

"Still no word on what's been happening, but we have had confirmation about the attack at the hotel. The man posing as a room-service waiter was identified as a member of Shearer's gang."

So they had found her, just as Miles had suspected.

He turned and watched Melissa through the picture window as she and Dylan sat with the family in the living room. He didn't want to keep living this secret with her, but how long could this charade go on? The threat would be looming over her as long as Shearer was alive. She would have to remain in WITSEC probably for the rest of her life, raising her son in the program just as she had been raised.

But that wasn't their most pressing issue. What they needed to know was how Shearer had found her in her last three locations including the hotel, which Griffin had checked out for himself, and how long it would take him to find her here at the ranch. That problem would only be solved by uncovering the leak in the marshals service.

Miles ended the call just as the front door opened and his sister stepped out onto the porch. "What are you doing out here all alone when your wife is inside?" Kellyanne asked.

He held up his phone, then slipped it back into his pocket. "Just a business call."

"Miles, you work too much. I am glad to see, though, that you made some time for love." She leaned against the rail and stared inside through the big picture window at Melissa. "I like her."

"I'm glad to hear that."

"I wish I'd been told about the wedding so I could have been a bridesmaid, but I do like her and I wish you both every happiness."

"Thank you."

"And I'm thrilled to finally be an aunt. I thought for sure Lawson and Bree would make me one first, but you beat them to it."

He stared at his brother Lawson and his new wife. Six months ago, she'd been the target of a group of drug runners her ex-boyfriend had crossed until Lawson and his brothers had taken them down and rescued both Bree and her twin sister. "How are they doing?"

"They're very happy. Daddy says they're leaving tomorrow for a horse auction. I think it's supposed to be like the honeymoon they never got to have."

"And why are you in town?"

She shrugged. "Just a little homesick is all. I took a few days off to rest and recharge over the holidays."

He sensed there was something more to her story, but he didn't ask. He didn't talk about his life or his job, and that meant he didn't have the right to push his siblings to do so, either. If she needed an ear, she knew he was there for her.

"I'd better get inside and rescue Melissa." He started

toward the door, but looked back at his sister and saw her watching him. As a social worker who worked with abused kids, she had an especially keen sense of when people were lying and he suspected she could tell when he was holding back. She'd never called him on it before, although she looked like she wanted to now.

He didn't give her the opportunity. He stepped inside and joined his fictional family as they helped finish decorating the Christmas tree. He lifted Dylan onto his shoulders so he could reach the top to place the star. It was a happy moment—lots of smiles, lots of hugs. But he couldn't help the feeling that when this was all over, no one in his real family would be able to forgive him.

When Miles first mentioned going horseback riding, Melissa hadn't been so sure about it, but as she looked into Dylan's face glowing with excitement, she couldn't refuse. Miles assured her he would be right there beside her the entire time, so she reluctantly let him lead her outside to the barn, where she climbed into the saddle.

"She's a good horse," Kellyanne assured her, stroking the horse's nose. "She's real gentle, too. You'll be fine."

Miles climbed onto his horse and grabbed the reins as Kellyanne lifted Dylan and placed him in front of Miles.

"Wait, I thought he would ride with me," Melissa argued.

"I'd rather wait and see how you handle the horse first," Miles told her.

Since she'd never been on a horse in her life, she

conceded that was probably a good idea. Miles had grown up around horses and knew how to ride. Dylan was probably much safer with him. In fact, she should probably just climb down and go back inside and read a book, but no matter how much she trusted Miles, she couldn't bring herself to let her child go off on a horse without her.

The thing was that she *did* trust Miles. She'd only known this man for a few days, yet it seemed like longer. She instinctively trusted him more than any of the other marshals she'd been placed with and she thought it was because he treated her like a person and not just a case number. One of the first marshals who'd been assigned to her had treated her like she was a criminal, either not knowing or simply not caring that she was an innocent victim in all of this. Miles was so different in his approach that it had helped her grow comfortable with him.

Don't get too comfortable, she reminded herself. But at the same time, she didn't want to be in a state of such hypertension that she failed to appreciate their wonderful surroundings. While they were here, Dylan would get to enjoy the fresh air and horses. It might be their only chance to go horseback riding in a long time.

Miles kept a slow pace with his horse and Melissa managed to keep up, getting used to riding her horse as they walked along. At first, she was so intense about concentrating on her seat that she missed the beauty of the countryside, but Dylan's squeals of excitement as he watched the birds and petted the horse pulled her back to the experience.

She enjoyed the feel of sunshine on her face, grateful that the afternoon weather was mild despite the December date on the calendar. Dylan wanted to pick some wildflowers that had blossomed in the warm temperatures, so Miles stopped and slid off the horse before lowering her son to the ground. Then he helped Melissa climb off, taking her by the waist and dropping her to the ground, but he held her just a moment longer than necessary before releasing her and hurrying off to chase Dylan. It had just been a moment, but she'd felt the connection between them, the mutual attraction, and knew it wasn't one-sided.

It was the first time she'd had a romantic thought about another man besides Vick. In a way, it felt good to know that that part of her wasn't completely gone. But on the other hand, she knew nothing could come of it. Her future wasn't here on the Silver Star Ranch with Miles. It was a new identity in a new town—and no contact with him ever again. She'd been telling herself not to let her son get too close to the handsome marshal when all along it should have been herself she'd been warning.

She was walking over to join them in picking flowers when a shot rang out.

The horses behind her bucked and jerked. Another shot rang out and Melissa felt something whiz past her.

Someone was shooting at her!

She dropped to the ground as Miles scooped up Dylan and ducked behind a tree. Then she watched him put down the boy and pull his gun.

"Stay low," he commanded her as he scanned the open area.

She had every intention of obeying, but the horses were agitated from the noise and she was fearful one of them would trample her. She rose to her feet to get away as another shot rang out. This time Miles returned fire and the horses took off running. She did, too, darting toward the cluster of trees where Miles and Dylan had taken cover.

She cleared the trees, then scooped up Dylan into her arms and hugged him to her as Miles continued firing.

"I think they're firing from that tree line," he said, motioning across the way. He stopped firing long enough to pull out his phone and call his brother Paul. "We're being shot at by someone in the tree line. We're on the south side of the lake. Come quick." He ended the call and turned his attention back to where the shots had come from.

"Did you see who was shooting?" she asked him.

"No, I didn't."

He didn't say so, but she could see from his stance and the way his shoulders hunched in concentration that this attack had him rattled. "It's them, isn't it?" She crouched to the ground with a whimpering Dylan.

"We don't know that for certain." He kneeled but remained in front of her and Dylan. "We have cover in the trees. We'll just wait for backup to arrive, then I want you to head back to the ranch while I go after whoever was doing the shooting."

She reached out to touch his arm. "Come back with us. Please, Miles."

"I can't. If our location has been compromised, I need to know it."

She heard an engine and looked to see a truck approaching them. Miles stood and motioned for her to do the same. As the truck came closer, she saw Paul and their father in it. John stopped the truck between the trees and the shooter, and Miles quickly ushered her and Dylan into the back seat as Paul exited and handed him a rifle.

She grabbed for his arm again. "Please come with us."

"We'll check it out and be back to the ranch soon," he promised.

"You're their father. Why don't you stop them?" she asked as John turned the truck around and headed back to the ranch house.

"They're grown men who know how to take care of themselves and each other. And if there's a threat to this ranch, we need to know about it. They're doing what needs to be done."

She clung to Dylan and tried to calm him down as she turned and glanced out the back window to see Miles and Paul chase down the horses, climb on them and then ride to the area where the shots had come from.

"I think the firing came from this direction," Miles said as he rode into the trees.

No shots had been fired for nearly ten minutes and Melissa was bound to be safely back at the ranch, so he was sure whoever had shot at them was long gone. Still, they needed to check it out.

"How many shots did you hear?" Paul asked.

"Three, all aimed in our direction."

"Could have been hunters on our land illegally. We had something similar happen back in the summer with someone firing at Lawson and Bree. You were here for that, weren't you?"

"Actually, I'd already left to return to work." But he remembered being told about it and wishing he'd remained at the ranch to help.

"Of course, in that case, it turned out to be drug dealers trying to kill Bree. Melissa doesn't have a drug ring after her, does she?"

He could tell his brother was kidding, but he shook his head. "No, not a drug ring."

Paul's joking demeanor vanished. "Who then?"

He shouldn't be sharing this info with his brother, but he wanted someone else to at least have an idea about the danger that might be lurking. And he trusted Paul completely. "Someone dangerous from her past. That's all I can say."

"Does he know she's here at the ranch?"

"I didn't think so, not until today."

Paul took off his cowboy hat, fiddled with it a moment then slid it back onto his head. "Well, it's probably nothing but stray bullets, but in case it's not, I'll ride over to the Simmons ranch. If someone entered our property here, they would have had to pass the Simmons ranch and they recently installed cameras."

"They did?" He'd told Melissa he knew this town

like the back of his hand, but he hadn't known about that development.

"Yep. Seems Mr. Simmons had a rash of vandalism on his property. Trees and fields damaged, fires set, so he installed those cameras. Found out his property had become a place where these college kids hung out at night and had their parties. He took the images to Josh and he shut them down the next night. Anyway, his cameras might help us figure out who drove this way." He climbed onto the horse and took off toward the Simmons ranch.

Miles hoped Paul found something because he didn't like not knowing for sure and he was lacking the resources he was accustomed to in order to figure things out. He kneeled down and looked at the ruts in the mud and the tire tracks. This didn't feel like stray bullets to him. Those shots had been too accurate to be accidental.

He pulled out his phone to call Griffin, but his hand hovered above the dial button. Griffin would tell him to pull out and find another safe house—and Miles wasn't ready to leave. He still thought being here was a good plan, even if he couldn't deny the fact that someone had been shooting at them.

He hit the button and dialed Griffin's number and when his boss answered, he spoke the words he didn't want to say.

"Our location may have been compromised."

FOUR

"Now hold on," Griffin stated. "Are you sure it was someone after Melissa?"

That was the problem. Miles wasn't sure about anything. The shots had seemed deliberate and targeted, but how could anyone have found them so quickly? It didn't make sense.

Griffin advised him to wait to gather more evidence before making any rash decisions and Miles decided he was right. He was jumping to conclusions, acting hastily because the fact that Melissa and Dylan had been found before had him rattled. Bad enough that he still didn't understand how they'd been discovered at the hotel. But *he'd* made these plans. No one connected with the marshals office, not even Griffin, knew where they were.

Miles returned to the house, where they all looked at him anxiously.

"What happened?" Kellyanne asked. "Did you find anything?"

He noticed Melissa was on the couch as Dylan

played at her feet. Her expression was one of anxiety and she must be wondering, like he was, if they'd been discovered and would have to leave.

"Paul went to the Simmons place to look at their video feed. He thinks it might have been stray bullets from illegal hunting."

His mother nodded, latching on to that explanation. "Yes, yes, that's probably right. We do get hunters this time of year."

"I'm just glad no one was hurt," his father stated, then promptly changed the topic. "Why don't we all get ready for some supper?"

Miles glanced at Melissa. He needed to get her alone and talk about this situation. "I think we're going to skip supper tonight, Mama."

Melissa stood. "Yes, I think that's for the best. I should really put Dylan down. It's been a long day." He liked how calm and collected she looked. She even smiled, though it didn't go to her eyes. None of them did. What would it look like to see her really smile? He wanted to make that happen someday.

His family didn't like the idea of them leaving but didn't put up much of an argument. Miles loaded Dylan into his car seat while Melissa climbed into the front. They were silent for several moments before she turned to him and asked the question he'd been expecting.

"Have we been discovered?"

He gripped the steering wheel. He wanted to reassure her, but he didn't want to mislead her. Honesty was the best option. "I'm not sure. I don't see how anyone could have discovered where you are. No one knows I'm even on the case, let alone that I brought you here."

"So you believe it might have just been an accident?"

He wanted to. He wanted to believe it so much. "The shots didn't seem accidental, but like I said, I don't know how anyone could have found us. I think it's too early to decide we've been discovered. My family is right. We do get hunters on the property this time of the season and Paul said the neighbors have been having trouble with kids trespassing to throw parties."

"So we're not leaving?"

"I don't want to go until we absolutely have to. I still believe you're both safe here."

He saw relief in her expression. "I'm glad. I like it here. It's a lot better than any other place we've been. I like your family, too, though I hate lying to them."

"It's necessary."

"I know it is and that's why I do it, but they'll be devastated when they discover the truth. They're already growing attached to Dylan and he to them."

His instinct was to reach across the seat and take her hand, but he didn't. That would be crossing a line. It was one thing to play the considerate husband in front of his family. It was another thing entirely while they were in private. Besides, it was better to keep his distance. He'd already gotten too close to the lovely brunette, was too admiring of her strength and determination.

He parked in front of the cabin and carried a sleeping Dylan inside, placing him on the bed. But he stood awkwardly in the doorway as she pulled a blanket over the boy and tucked him in for the night before leaning down to plant a kiss on his forehead. This woman was amazing in so many ways. She kept her calm in the face of danger and plastered a smile on her face for his family. It took a lot of strength to keep up the charade that everything was fine when her world was crumbling around her.

"Are you two going to be okay?" He wasn't ready to leave them alone and that surprised him. He had stuff to do—make certain their cover was still intact, check the perimeter, follow up with both his brother and Griffin—but his feet were planted in this doorway with this little family that reminded him of everything he'd ever wanted.

"We'll be okay," she said, but she didn't seem to be in any hurry for him to leave, either. She wasn't pushing him away. "I did enjoy the horse ride. So did Dylan. Thank you for doing that."

"You're welcome. It didn't turn out to be as much fun as I'd hoped."

"Dylan had a good time."

She crossed her arms over her body and he sensed the fear she'd kept pushed down was starting to resurface.

Despite his determination to keep his distance, he reached out and stroked her arm. "Everything is going to be okay, Melissa. I won't let anything happen to you or Dylan."

A tear slipped from her eye and she wiped it away. "I think I'm just tired. Tired of all the running and the hiding and deceit. Today, for just a moment, I let my guard down and enjoyed myself. I want to be able to do that again. I don't want to live my life looking over my shoulder, constantly on guard, the way my mother did. And I don't want my son to have to live that way."

No one should have to live that way, but he couldn't change the way the world worked. His job was to make sure she was safe and that often meant constantly being on guard. But she was right. It was no way to live. He would do his best to ensure that wherever she wound up was secure and no one could find her. She might still carry some fear, but hopefully, someday, she'd feel safe again. He'd watched her today when she'd let go and had fun. He'd enjoyed seeing her that way, and he wanted to see her really smile, the kind of smile he imagined made the golden specks in her brown eyes shine. That was the kind of life he hoped for her and Dylan.

He said good-night and left her. She didn't need him to see her falling apart. She needed her privacy. It was his job to keep her safe, not comfort her...despite how much he longed to do so.

A knock at the door had him reaching for his weapon. He kept it hidden while he glanced through the peephole and spotted his brother Paul. He tucked the gun back into its holster and opened the door, anxious to hear what his brother had discovered.

Paul walked inside and glanced around. "Where's Melissa?"

"She's already gone to bed. What did you find?"

Paul pulled out his phone and showed him surveillance-camera images of a pickup that pulled into the clearing between the Simmons ranch and their property. "It's definitely two young guys, can't be older than early twenties. I had Josh run the truck's tags and he recognized the names immediately as some college kids he's run from the property before for illegal hunting."

"You think that's all this was? Illegal hunting?"

"It seems likely." He slipped his phone into his pocket. "Unless you want to give me more information about whoever it is that's after Melissa."

He wished he'd never said anything to Paul, especially if it really turned out to be nothing more than stray bullets from these kids hunting illegally on their property.

"It's nothing. I shouldn't have even said anything."

Paul shot him a look to let him know he didn't believe him, but he didn't push the matter, probably figuring that Miles would share when he was ready. But he wasn't going to share. He couldn't. Not when it meant putting his family and Melissa in even greater danger.

Paul left and Miles checked the perimeter then locked up. He fell into a chair and pushed a hand through his hair as the events of the day caught up to him. He'd overreacted and it had nearly cost them their safe house. He should have remembered about the illegal hunting problems that were an ongoing issue in the area. He sent off a quick text to Griffin that he thought they were safe after all.

He took comfort in knowing that he'd done everything he could to protect Melissa and that no one should be able to connect them, or find her here. She was safe at Silver Star, safe with him and his family.

Early the next morning, Miles drove Melissa and Dylan back to the main house for breakfast with the family. It was Sunday and that meant all the Averys loaded up for church. Melissa had been a good sport about going when Miles had mentioned it. He'd offered to make up an excuse, but she'd assured him she didn't mind going.

He parked in front of the house and wasn't surprised to see activity already happening in the barn. Ranch work demanded an early start. It was one thing he hadn't missed about being home.

His phone buzzed and he glanced at the screen, noticing Lanie's number on the caller ID. "I need to take this. I'll meet you inside," he told Melissa, who took Dylan and walked into the house.

He answered, expecting to hear Lanie's voice, but instead heard two voices—Lanie's and Adam's. "We're just here having breakfast together," Adam told him. "You're missing out on doughnuts and coffee."

"Griffin told us about your dad's relapse," Lanie added. "We wanted to call and see if there was anything we could do."

"I appreciate the offer. He's doing a little better, but I'm going to stick around the ranch until he's one hundred percent."

"That makes sense," Lanie said. "Give him our love and let us know if we can help in any way."

He thanked them both, then hung up and put away his phone. Lying to his best friends left a sour taste in his mouth. Lanie and Adam had always been the ones he didn't have to keep secrets from and that had been special to him. Now, everything had changed.

Miles spotted an unfamiliar face working on a piece of equipment and walked over to check him out. He was young, probably no more than seventeen or eighteen, but Miles didn't recognize him. "What's your name?" he asked the boy.

"Luke Mitchell." The boy reached out to shake his hand but Miles hesitated. He didn't know him or what Luke was doing working on this piece of equipment.

Paul came around the corner and greeted Miles. "I see you've met Luke."

"I did." Miles pulled his brother aside. "What's he doing here?"

"He's one of the kids Josh and Lawson are mentoring and training to work on a ranch. They're hoping by giving them ranching skills, they'll stay out of trouble."

He wasn't thrilled at hearing his brothers were letting juvenile delinquents onto the property, especially with Melissa and Dylan around. "When did this start?"

"They've been talking about doing it for a while, but last month they converted that old shed behind the barn into a bunkhouse and Josh picked four boys for the program."

"Do you think it's a good idea to let criminals, even kid criminals, around?"

"They're just kids, Miles. None of them are violent offenders. They got in over their heads and need some help straightening themselves out. I think Josh just wants to do whatever he can to keep them out of juvenile detention. Besides, so far, they've all been good workers. Especially Luke over there. He has a real knack for mechanical work. It seems to come naturally to him."

He glanced at Luke, who was also eyeing him with

suspicion. Miles still didn't like it. He hadn't antici-
pated having extra people hanging around the Silver
Star when he'd brought Melissa and Dylan here. But
it wasn't really his place to tell anyone they couldn't
stay. The Silver Star might be his childhood home, but
Josh and Lawson lived here permanently and Paul had
been living here during his recuperation from his injuries sustained in a Special Forces operation.

He motioned toward the stables. There seemed to
be several new horses he didn't recognize also. "These
are new, too. Lots of changes around here in the past
few months."

Paul shook his head. "These aren't ours. We're just
caring for them. They belong to the Woodwards, but
Clint isn't able to look after them right now."

He remembered the Woodwards as a nice couple
who'd purchased a ranch closer to town several years
ago. A lot of their neighbors had been having a hard
time keeping their ranches going. "What happened to
them?"

"Their barn caught fire. Clint ran inside to free the
horses. They all survived, but he suffered burns. He's
still in a recovery center in Dallas, but even after he
gets home, I doubt he'll be able to take care of them for
a while. I'm hoping one of these boys will be willing to
help him out until he gets back on his feet."

Miles was sorry to hear about Clint Woodward. He
remembered him as being a nice guy. "How did the fire
start? Lightning strike?"

Paul shook his head. "Nope. The fire marshal says it
was purposely set. There have been a string of arsons in

the area. Four in the past nine months. Unfortunately, Josh and his investigators haven't found the perpetrator. The other ranchers have been able to rebuild, but Clint's injuries make it unlikely he'll be able to."

"I'm sorry to hear that." He stroked the nose of one of the horses. "They're fine animals."

"They were traumatized by the fire. Lawson has been working with them, but they still spook easily. It's going to take some time for them to fully recover, too." He motioned toward the mare at the end. "Plus, this one is pregnant. The vet has been keeping a close eye on her since the fire."

He didn't like the idea that an unknown arsonist was operating in the area, but he knew that wherever he took Melissa, there were always going to be criminals around. That was just the way of the world. It didn't mean they posed any threat to his witness or to his family. And in this particular case, he was glad his family had been there to reach out to the Woodwards.

He nodded at Luke Mitchell, who continued to shoot him an accusatory stare. He was probably as unhappy to see a stranger asking questions about him as Miles was at having a stranger around. He still didn't feel great about having four juveniles he didn't know hanging around, but his brothers were on a mission to mentor and teach them. He couldn't fault Josh and Lawson for that, especially when it had been his choice not to be around. He had left the ranch behind years before to focus on his career.

He glanced back at the house and spotted Melissa through the window. At least he hadn't had his entire life turned upside down the way she had. His problems paled in comparison to those of Melissa and her son. He had no reason to complain, even if it saddened him to realize that his existence was empty. Work was all he had and he wanted so much more. He wanted a wife and a family. But that kind of family life didn't appear to be an option for him.

"It's good to have you home for Christmas," Paul stated. "I know Mom and Dad are glad you are here. So am I."

"I'm glad to be here. Glad I—" he remembered he was supposed to be married and rephrased "—*we* can be here." He saw Paul glancing at him and felt the need to explain himself. "My job often keeps me away."

"You don't have to explain that to me. It's been a few years since I've been home for Christmas. Lawson and Bree will be home on Christmas Eve and Kellyanne is hanging around until New Year's. If Colby was here, Mom and Dad would have the whole family together." Their brother Colby was an FBI agent and, like Miles, often gone for work.

Miles took comfort that his secret assignment would bring his parents a good bit of enjoyment during Christmas…at least until it was time to leave.

After a family breakfast, Miles and Melissa returned to the cabin to change for church. She made do with a dress she'd borrowed from Kellyanne and made certain Dylan looked presentable.

Miles appeared, clean-shaven and with his hair still wet from his shower. He was wearing a suit and tie with his cowboy boots and she felt herself flush, thinking how well he cleaned up.

"Are you sure you don't mind going to church with my family?" he asked. His insistent questioning made her wonder if he wanted her to give him an excuse to skip the service, but she wasn't going to do that. Going was the least he could do for his parents, especially given the whopper of a secret they were keeping from them.

She moved toward him and straightened his tie. "Growing up, my mother had me in church every time the doors opened."

He smiled. "Same here. Do you still attend church as an adult?"

"I did. After Vick died, I had no one but my mother to lean on. God was my strength during that time. But now… He seems so far away. What about you? Do you still attend as an adult?"

He shook his head. "Not regularly. I'm a member of a church, but my job keeps me away so frequently that no one blinks if I miss several weeks in a row. But I'm there so irregularly that there's no connection there to anyone."

He shrugged like it was no big deal, but Melissa felt for him. Without her faith, she wouldn't have made it through pulling her life back together after Vick's death. But it was her mother who had been her real strength. Now, she was gone, too.

He glanced at his watch. "We should get going. We'll meet them at the house and follow them into town."

Melissa was nervous by the time Miles pulled into

the church parking lot. She'd grown up with her faith and it had meant a lot to her, but now with everything that was happening—her mother's death, them running for their lives and living in secret and danger—she was questioning everything, including God's presence in her life.

Where was He and why had He allowed this to happen to her?

She walked inside with Miles. Word had obviously spread about their marriage, and everyone crowded around to wish them well. She accepted the congratulations, but she felt wrong just being here, lying to everyone. The people they met were welcoming and Melissa wished her real life was this way. Even before the revelation of her mother's past, she hadn't had any close friends. Her mother had always frowned on her getting too close to anyone. Now, Melissa understood why she'd been the way she had, but she'd promised herself that Dylan would grow up differently, that she would get him involved in social activities. She'd hoped to be the one with the house where he and his friends wanted to play. A tear slipped from her cheek. That would never happen now. She would end up raising Dylan just as her mother had raised her—overly cautious, because they would have to be. His life depended on her keeping him close and viewing others with suspicion.

She took a seat with the family and Miles's hand on her back was a relief. They were only pretending to be married, but she found comfort in the gesture. She felt safe with him. Safe and protected. And it only served to reinforce how different this life was from what she was entering into.

She wiped away a tear that slipped from her eye. She was already crying and the service hadn't even started yet. How was she ever going to explain that?

The music was wonderfully soothing and she leaned into the melody of it. She missed God, missed the closeness she used to share with Him, but that had all been based on a lie, hadn't it? How could God ever bless a secret life, a lying life?

Dylan shifted and fidgeted and Miles's father pulled him into his lap and comforted him. He settled down quickly enough. She was ever so thankful for this family that had taken her in, but she wondered what would happen when they discovered it was all a lie. Dylan was becoming close with them, as they were with him. They believed they finally had a grandchild and she and Miles would soon take that away from them. What a heartless and cruel thing to do.

She sat down and listened to the preacher and her heart ached. She longed to feel the Holy Spirit moving, but God seemed so far away from her now. Since her mother's murder, her old faith seemed hollow and naive. God wasn't there. Not for her, not anymore.

When the service ended, she excused herself and walked to the ladies' room. She splashed cold water on her face and tried to rein in the emotions the service had stirred in her. She couldn't fall apart. She had to remain strong for Dylan. She wiped her face and smoothed down her hair, but the wedding ring on her finger glinted in the light, a reminder that she was lying to everyone she'd met today, even the pastor. All those well-wishers from earlier had been deceived and she didn't deserve their friendliness. When the truth came out, they would all know they'd been misled.

Suddenly the hairs on her neck rose as she sensed someone nearby. She saw no one in the mirror but still spun around. She pushed open each stall door. No one was there. The restroom was empty except for her. Why then did she still feel eyes on her, watching her?

She rubbed away the goose bumps on her arm. She was just being paranoid. No one was there. No one was watching her, yet she couldn't shake the feeling until she was back in the SUV with Miles on the drive to the restaurant where they were going to have a family lunch. He reached across the seat for her hand and held it, and she liked the way her hand felt wrapped in his.

"You seemed pretty emotional back there. I guess that's to be expected."

"I hate this," she told him. "I hate the lying and deception. It doesn't feel right."

He pulled his hand away and she regretted her words. She hadn't meant to sound as if she was criticizing him or the way he was handling things. She felt safer with Miles than she had since this entire nightmare had started.

"I'm just anxious," she confessed. "I'm worried about all of this."

"I know you are, but I'm not going to allow anyone to harm you or Dylan. That's a promise."

She appreciated him saying so, but she knew he might not be able to keep that promise. She'd been found before, three times, and her and her son's lives had been in danger over and over again. What made this time so different?

"Being on the ranch means I can protect you and Dylan a lot better. I trust my family, Melissa. You're safe here."

She wanted to believe him, because she loved being here—and so did Dylan. He was starting to remind her of his old self, how he'd behaved before this nightmare began, and they'd only been here a few days.

But this would all be over too soon. They would be transferred to another place, another city, another marshal, and Dylan would once again be traumatized. She wondered if they would be here for Christmas and what a Christmas celebration with a family like the Averys would be like.

The tree in the corner of the living room was twice as big as any she'd ever had and the lights and decorations were amazing. This family took Christmas seriously and not just the gift-giving part. They celebrated the real reason for Christmas, the birth of Christ, just as she had with her mother. The two celebrations were different in the particulars, but similar in that aspect.

How had her mother done it? How had she had such faith after all she'd been through?

Miles parked and she unbuckled Dylan from his car seat before following him into the restaurant, where his family was waiting. His mother was so busy with projects for the upcoming Christmas banquet at the church that she didn't have time to make Sunday supper, as usual, so the family had chosen to eat out. Melissa joined them, taking a seat beside Miles as Kellyanne took Dylan from her arms and buckled him into a booster seat beside her. Miles's sister was getting so attached to Dylan and while she was pleased for the attention for her son, she worried about the aftereffect once they were gone. Kellyanne would be heartbroken to learn this marriage had all been a ruse and Dylan wasn't, in fact, her nephew.

She hated to think that these people would be punished for being kind and welcoming. If they'd been less open, less eager to accept her, they wouldn't be as hurt by her leaving and taking Dylan with her. They were good people. She could tell in the way they watched out for one another and treated her and Dylan as family, despite their absolute disbelief when they'd learned Miles had gotten married without telling them. Strangely, she realized that none of them seemed too surprised by his actions once they'd calmed down from the initial shock. Based on her conversations with Kellyanne and Mrs. Avery, it seemed that Miles was known to be aloof and extremely private. Of course, she understood his reasoning for not telling his parents or his siblings about his work, but it was a little surprising to hear that his family accepted him as he was without a need for explanation. Had this man always been so stoic and unassuming? And how was it possible that someone so handsome didn't stand out in a crowd? She supposed it had to do with his training. In his job, the less he stood out, the more protected his witnesses were.

A chill rushed through her and she shuddered and rubbed her arms.

Miles slid his arm behind her and leaned toward her. "Are you okay?"

She nodded. "Just a sudden chill."

She tried to give him a reassuring smile, but the same feeling of being watched suddenly besieged her again. She glanced around. The restaurant was crowded and anyone could be looking her way. She scooted her chair closer to Miles. She couldn't explain the feeling and couldn't see anyone watching them, but she felt the angry, bitter stare burrowing into her.

Miles put his arm around her. "You're shaking. What's the matter?"

Her chin quivered and she felt silly. "I don't know. I just… I feel like someone is watching me."

He glanced around the restaurant, then leaned in to whisper in her ear. "I'm going to have a look around. Don't worry. You're safe here at the table with my family." He stood and excused himself, then walked off. Paul and Josh followed him a moment later.

Kellyanne looked surprised when they left. "What do you think that's about?" she asked her parents.

"I have no idea," her mother commented.

"I'm sure it's nothing," her father said, shrugging away the issue. He seemed to have an easy faith in his children.

Melissa reached for her glass and pretended to sip it, hoping Kellyanne wouldn't look to her for an explanation. She didn't. Instead, she turned back to giggle at Dylan, who was making a mess with a bowl of mashed potatoes.

Miles and Paul returned to the table several minutes later.

"Josh got called to work," Miles told the table. "Something about a bad wreck out on the highway."

"Oh, dear, I hope no one was injured," Mrs. Avery said. "We'll wrap up his meal and take it home with us. He can reheat it later if he likes."

And with that, the conversation turned to something else.

Melissa leaned into Miles and whispered in his ear. "What did you find?"

"Nothing. You're perfectly safe."

She turned back to her meal, realizing how silly she was being. Of course, she was safe. No one could possibly know where she was or who she was with. She'd never felt as secure as she did at the Silver Star with Miles. She chalked up her fears to lingering paranoia. She'd been on guard for weeks. It was normal that she was having trouble adjusting now.

And that probably explained why her delicious meal tasted bland in her mouth.

FIVE

Miles spotted his brother Josh waiting for him on the front porch when they returned to the Silver Star. He motioned toward Miles as he parked.

"Why don't you take Dylan and go into the house," he suggested to Melissa. He didn't take his eyes off her and Dylan until they were inside. Then he turned to his brother.

Josh stepped off the porch and headed for the barn, away from the house, and Miles followed him. "We were able to track down the two men from the video. Twenty-two-year-old Michael Davis and twenty-one-year-old Steven Gideon. I had Cecile bring them into the station and interview them about their activities yesterday afternoon."

Miles nodded. Cecile was Josh's chief deputy in his office, and Miles knew her to be extremely competent in her duties.

His brother continued. "They both claimed they were on the property for hunting and had no intention of shooting anyone."

Miles was relieved at the innocent explanation and once again wished he hadn't jumped to conclusions. "Thank you, Josh. And thank Cecile for me, too."

"This isn't the first time either of them has been ticketed for illegal trespassing. They have four incidents between them, so they'll each have to pay a hefty fine. Beyond that, I don't think there's anything to worry about, but I'm happy to delve further into their lives if you think this has something to do with whoever is after Melissa."

Miles grimaced as Josh revealed he knew about the danger Melissa was in.

Josh shrugged. "Paul told me. I wish *you* had told me."

"It's nothing."

"It must be something. You've been edgy and cautious ever since you arrived home. Whatever it is, we can help. We want to help."

He pulled a hand through his hair. He hadn't meant to alarm his brothers and he certainly didn't need them looking into anything. But keeping them on alert for potential hazards might be helpful.

He guarded his words, careful not to give too much away. His WITSEC involvement was still a secret from his family and he intended to keep it that way. "Melissa's mother was killed a few weeks ago. She was shot in her home. Melissa walked in on the shooter and barely escaped herself."

"So she can identify him?"

"Yes, she can. The killer managed to escape and he's still on the loose. I don't believe she's in any immediate danger because I don't believe he can track her here, but you can understand that we're both a little on edge."

"I'm sorry to hear about her mother."

"Thank you. I overreacted to the shots being fired."

"I understand why you would, but don't you think this is something you should have told me? If Melissa is a target, I can help protect her."

"I do have a few skills in that area myself, Josh. I'm perfectly capable of keeping her safe."

"I know you can. I didn't mean to step on your toes, Miles. I only want to help and I am the sheriff."

"Thank you, but it's not necessary. And I would appreciate it if you didn't mention this to anyone else, either. Melissa is trying to make the best of things for Dylan's sake."

Josh nodded. "Understood."

He left his brother and walked inside, a little miffed at Paul for mentioning anything to Josh. He knew his brothers were there for him if he needed them—that was part of his reasoning for bringing her here. But he wasn't looking to pull his family into this situation any further than they already were. As long as Melissa's identity was hidden, he wouldn't need the extra protection they were offering.

He called his boss again on the way to the house to let him know their location had not been compromised, after all. Griffin was glad to hear it but had no update on locating the mole in WITSEC.

"I've come across several marshals who've made some large purchases lately, but I haven't had time to check them out to make sure they're legitimate."

Large purchases could be a result of accepting some bribe money. "Like who?"

"Well, Lanie, for one. Did you know she just put a large down payment on an expensive new house?"

Miles rubbed his face at that news. He'd heard her decry living in the city more times than he could count, but he hadn't heard anything about buying a new house. Why wouldn't she have mentioned that? And where had she gotten the money?

"I'll let you know if I find anything."

Griffin ended the call, and Miles slipped his phone into his pocket. He couldn't believe Lanie could be a mole. There was probably a perfectly legitimate explanation for where she'd gotten the money to purchase that house. Part of him wanted to call her up and demand an answer, but he checked that response. That wasn't his job—and it might interfere with Griffin's investigation. Miles's job was to protect Melissa and Dylan. Griffin would handle the rest.

But as he recalled the way Melissa had shuddered in fear and leaned into him, he realized he was already taking her safety too personally. She was a beautiful, strong, determined woman and it was his duty to protect her and her son. It wasn't his job to enjoy getting so close, or to notice the sweet scent of her shampoo.

Melissa helped Dylan out of his jacket and boots. She'd enjoyed the day so far with Miles's family, but as she glanced out the window and spotted him huddled near the barn with his brother, she wondered what they were discussing.

She couldn't concentrate on that. She had to keep her mind on something else and keep Dylan occupied, as well. "What should we do this afternoon?" she asked him. "Would you like to watch a Christmas movie?"

Kellyanne approached them. "Actually, I promised Dylan we would do a Christmas craft this afternoon."

"That sounds like fun. What are we making?"

But Dylan pushed her away. "No, you can't see, Mama."

Kellyanne's face turned red. "I told him we would make a surprise for you. I hope you don't mind."

"Not at all."

She was glad to see Dylan looking so happy and having a good time. She chose to focus on that, and not on how hard it would be for all of them when they had to part ways.

Having been shooed away by her three-year-old son, Melissa ventured into the kitchen, where Diane had pulled on her apron and was preparing for an afternoon of baking. Melissa recognized the signs from having watched her mother do the same thing many times.

Tears pressed against her eyes at the familiar sight. It was a different kitchen and a different woman, but she saw her own mother standing and laughing in the kitchen while baking cookies for her and Dylan's Christmas party.

"Melissa, what's wrong?"

She quickly wiped away a tear that had spilled down her cheek and pasted on a smile. "Nothing. I'm fine."

Diane took her arm and pulled out a chair for her to sit. "Something is wrong. You've gone positively pale, and don't think I don't see those tears, no matter how hard you're fighting to hold them back. I know you think you need to be strong for Dylan, honey—but it's just the two of us in here. You can talk to me."

She wiped away the tears that streamed down her face. "It's nothing. I—I just… My mother loved to bake. She had just started a home baking business. On the day she died the house smelled of cookies she'd been baking as a Christmas present for the employees at Dylan's day care."

Diane placed a hand on her shoulder. "I'm sorry. That must have been jarring for you. Is this your first Christmas without her?"

She nodded. These people had no idea how fresh and raw her mother's death was, or how unresolved her feelings were when it came to everything surrounding it. She wasn't supposed to talk about it, but she couldn't push away the memory of that smell and then finding her mother dead. Holiday baking would never be the same.

Diane turned back to her preparation while Melissa watched. She probably expected her to jump up and run off, and part of her wanted to do that, but the other part, the part that missed her mom so much, just wanted to sit and bask in the aroma. "She always smelled like warm bread," she told Diane. "Most moms smell like perfume or lotion, but my mother always smelled like freshly baked bread."

"I take it you and she were close?"

"Oh, yes, we were very close. When my husband, Vick, was killed, she was right there for us, letting us move in with her so she could help me raise Dylan. She was my rock." She wiped away another tear as she realized she'd depended on her mom for so many things and that, in turn, her mother had freely given Melissa everything—everything except the truth.

"My mother was the one who instilled in me the love of cooking," Diane said. "But baking is my favorite thing to do. I find comfort in it and I enjoy seeing how a cupcake or a cookie can bring a smile to someone's face."

Melissa smiled, her estimation of Miles's mother growing. "I think you and my mom would have gotten along."

"Thank you. I take that as a compliment. I've got three dozen cookies to bake for our annual Christmas banquet. I would love the help if you think you're up to it."

Melissa thought that would be a proper way to honor her mom and appreciated the offer. "I'd like that," she said, wiping away her tears and pulling on an apron that Diane handed her.

Christmas just wouldn't be Christmas without the familiar scent of cookies baking in the oven. She wouldn't let the negative associations haunt her—not when the good memories so heavily outweighed the bad. This was the way her mother would want to be remembered…and celebrated.

His mother was waiting on the porch for him when Miles approached the house. "I wanted to speak to you about Melissa. She was so upset earlier. Are you aware this will be her first Christmas without her mom?"

"I am." But he'd given no thought to how she was handling it. WITSEC was hard enough, but to have to deal with Christmas and a pretend family, too, must have been an extraordinary burden on her. He'd been so consumed with keeping her and Dylan safe that he hadn't even thought about how much being around his family would make her miss her mom. She hadn't even had time to really grieve for her and here he was shoving his family at her.

Knucklehead.

He had to do better.

"She's suffering a lot," his mom said. "You need to be considerate of that."

"I will," he promised, then kissed her, thankful to still have her. It was just like his mom to be thinking of others during their times of need. They'd nearly lost his dad earlier in the year, so that put some perspective on how he viewed losing a parent. How would he feel if his dad had died and he'd immediately been forced to basically forget about him? He was sure that he wouldn't have handled it very well, but Melissa was holding up like a trouper. He knew she was doing her best to be strong for Dylan's sake, and he believed she was doing an amazing job of it. Too amazing. All that grief had to go somewhere, and he hated the thought of her hiding it, crying in the bathroom or in her bed at night rather than allowing herself to admit she needed comfort.

He wanted to do something nice for her to help her get past this, but there wasn't much he could do.

He couldn't have a service or a ceremony. In fact, he shouldn't even be talking about her mom's recent death with anyone, let alone his mother. Hopefully, the circumstances of her mother's death hadn't been mentioned.

They spent a quiet afternoon with the family and by the time it grew dark outside, Dylan had fallen asleep in Melissa's lap. He was covered in glitter and clutching a star he'd made out of Popsicle sticks. Melissa rubbed his hair and glanced at him with so much love. Miles couldn't imagine loving someone so much that it elicited that kind of look, but he wanted that so much. He wanted to be a father, a husband—wanted to share his life with someone and build a family—but he knew he couldn't count on achieving those goals.

Especially since he was starting to want *this* family, and that definitely wasn't an option.

Melissa raised her head and looked at him, startling him with her intuition. Could she sense how focused he'd been on her?

He got up, walked to the couch and held out his hand. "I want to show you something."

His dad stood and offered his help. "I'll take Dylan upstairs and put him down while you go with Miles."

She handed Dylan off to Miles's dad then reached for his hand and stood to face him. "Where are we going?"

"Someplace special." He grabbed both of their coats and led them outside to the barn. He pushed open the main door and walked through to the center, where he reached for the ladder that led up to the hayloft.

She balked when he pulled it down. "I'm not sure about this, Miles."

They only used this area for storage, but it had the most beautiful view of the countryside. "It'll be great. Trust me." He held out his hand and after a moment of hesitation, she took it. That meant a lot to him. It told him she did trust him.

He climbed the ladder first then helped her up. The loft was dark and stuffy, and she coughed several times at the dust. He could tell that she wasn't terribly impressed so far, but he knew once the doors were opened that her opinion would change. He used the flashlight on his phone to light the way to the doors and unlatched them, swinging one and then the other open.

Melissa gasped and moved closer to him. The view did not disappoint. It was a cloudless night and the dark sky was lit up with bright, shining stars above them and clear country landscape ahead of them. Below, several horses neighed in the corral, but otherwise the night was still and silent.

He took her hand again and led her toward the edge, then sat down and pulled her beside him. She let her legs hang over the side and leaned into him, and he soaked in the scent of her hair. He couldn't express in words why he'd wanted to share this view with her, wanted her to love this place just as he did, but he did. He shouldn't want it. Shouldn't be getting so close to her and caring so much about her. But the pull of her overpowered his instincts to keep his distance.

"It's so beautiful," she said, staring from the sky to him. Her brown eyes shone with delight and it was all he could do to stop himself from putting his arms around her and pulling her into a kiss.

He turned away, knowing his actions would only result in heartbreak. Their lives were on two different paths and she'd already made it clear that she could never be with someone with so many secrets. Besides, his growing feelings for her were already clouding his judgment and he could not allow that to happen. Her safety, and Dylan's safety, were too important to him.

So instead of kissing, they talked. They actually ended up talking for over an hour. She queried him about what it was like for him growing up here on the ranch and why he'd felt he had to leave it.

"The world was calling to me. I knew I wanted to help people. I knew I wanted to do something that I would never find here."

She shook her head. "If I'd grown up here, I don't think I ever would have left."

"This place is important to me. It's my home and it always will be. But it's not where my life is any longer. I love what I do. I love being a part of something bigger than myself and helping bring people to justice."

She snuggled against him and placed her head on his shoulder. "You're a protector at heart. I knew it the first time I met you. I am thankful you decided to leave this ranch and join the marshals service. Who knows what would have happened to Dylan and me if we'd been left in someone else's charge."

"There are plenty of good people with the marshals who would have done anything in their power to keep you and Dylan safe."

"Maybe, but it wouldn't have been you and I can't imagine trusting anyone else as much as I trust you, Miles."

She looked at him and he saw that trust and vulnerability in her face. She was putting all of her faith in him and his skills, and he didn't want to let her down. He wanted to be the one she could trust without doubt, without fear. But how could he keep her safe when there was so much he didn't understand about the threats against her? And, more important, how was he ever going to be able to let her go once the threats against her were neutralized?

He heard movement below and figured one of his brothers was giving the horses their final check for the night. "It's getting late. We should get back to the house," he said and she nodded.

"And I need to check on Dylan."

He stood, then helped her to her feet. Her hand fit perfectly inside his and a rush of electricity sped up his arm at her touch. She must have felt it, too, because she leaned into him and lifted her head to look at him. He saw in her face everything he wanted out of life. A wife. A family. A companion to share his life with. He lowered his face to hers and felt the excitement between them. None of the obstacles between them mattered in this moment, as he held her in his arms. He touched his lips to hers and felt her give beneath him as he kissed her, his mind racing only with thoughts about her and the way she made him feel.

She broke the kiss but didn't pull away. One of his hands rested on her cheek, his finger curving under her jaw far enough to feel the racing beat of her pulse under his finger. It matched his own accelerated pulse.

"I can't breathe," she said, but she still didn't move away. Instead, her eyes searched his.

He was having a difficult time breathing himself and the temperature seemed to have shot up. She had that effect on him.

Then he realized, the breathlessness they were feeling wasn't from the kiss or the charged atmosphere between them.

Smoke filled the loft from the trapdoor they'd used to climb up into the loft. He ran to it and glanced down into the barn. Fire blazed upward, consuming the ladder as the horses, still in their stalls, whinnied and kicked, trying to escape the flames.

In the distance, footsteps rushed toward the barn and he recognized his brothers' voices as they entered the burning barn and started opening stalls and forcing out the animals.

Melissa stood over him. "What are we going to do?"

He pushed her away from the opening as flames shot up and the ladder finally caved, crashing to the floor. "We can't get out that way." He rushed to the edge of the loft and glanced down. There was nothing soft for them to land on if they jumped. In fact, a piece of farm equipment was parked directly below, making a jump all the more dangerous.

Panic filled Melissa's face and he suspected she was thinking about Dylan and never seeing him again. He took her shoulders and locked eyes with her. "We'll figure out how to get out of here. I promise."

He turned and hollered out for his brothers, hoping one of them could hear him over the roar of the fire and the noises the horses were making. He spotted Paul and Luke and two other kids he didn't recognize, who must have been the others from the teen mentoring group. Yet none of them seemed to hear his calls for help.

He took out his cell phone and dialed Paul's number. He watched his brother reach for the phone, hoping and praying he wouldn't be so focused on the emergency in front of him that he'd let it go to voice mail.

Paul pulled out his phone, seemed to check the caller ID then answered the call. "Miles, I'm—"

"We're trapped in the loft," he said, cutting off his brother.

Paul turned and glanced up. His face hardened as he spotted them.

"The ladder burned up," Miles continued. "We're trapped. We need a way down."

Paul glanced around, then started shouting for help to move the hay baler away from the barn. Two of the ranch hands tried to move it, but it was apparently hot to the touch from its proximity to the fire, because they had to slip out of their coats and use them as gloves in order to move the equipment.

Melissa screamed and Miles spun around to see the loft floor giving way under her feet. He grabbed her before the floor fell away. He pulled her to him and moved closer to the loft opening. The fire was spreading quickly and he smelled gasoline in the flames. This was no accident. Someone had intentionally set this fire.

"Hang on," Paul shouted, as the boys helped him carry hay bales beneath the loft.

"We have to jump," he said, knowing the hay wouldn't last long this close to the fire.

She shook her head as fear made her stiff and unyielding. "I can't. It's too far."

"They can't move the bales any closer to the barn because they would burn up. This is our only chance to get out, Melissa. We don't have much longer before this floor gives way completely." Already the fire had climbed the walls and was engulfing the roof. Soon they would have to worry about that giving, too. They couldn't stay here.

"Think about Dylan. You have to get to him."

That seemed to get to her and she turned to face the opening, but just when he thought she was going to step off the ledge, she stopped and turned back to him, kissing him hard on the lips before leaping off the edge. She screamed but landed in the hay and Paul scrambled to pull her to safety, then motioned for Miles to jump, too.

He glanced back at the roof as it collapsed around him. He nearly didn't make it in time but he jumped an instant before the debris had a chance to hit him. He landed hard, only half on the hay bale, and jammed his arm, pain spearing through him. Paul didn't waste any time pulling him to his feet and he had no choice but to scramble, too, and move with his brother, ignoring the pain. More distance from the fire was a necessity—and it couldn't wait. If he didn't move now, a busted shoulder would be the least of his concerns.

The heat from the barn was immense and he felt the

difference in temperature the farther away he got. At the house, he spotted Melissa being tended to by his mother and he hurried to her. She saw him and horror filled her face, probably at the soot and hay that covered him.

"Miles!" She pushed away the blanket his mother offered her and ran to him, slamming into his sore shoulder. He ignored the pain that shot through his injured arm and pulled his good one around her, thankful she was safe, thankful they *both* were safe.

A loud crack from behind him caused him to turn to see the barn, now fully engulfed in flames, as it crumbled under the weight and imploded on itself. Paul and the others did their best to fight the blaze—not to save the structure, but to keep the fire from spreading. Miles figured it would be a losing battle to salvage any part of the barn given the gasoline he'd smelled, but their priority had to be to contain it. The barn would be a total loss, but at least he saw that what looked like all of the horses had been rescued.

His father approached him and hugged both him and Melissa tightly. "Are you both okay?"

He nodded and so did she.

"How did this happen? Did you see anything?"

He shook his head, realizing that while he had been distracted kissing Melissa, someone had been watching them and setting a fire that nearly cost her and his family dearly. They'd lost so much with the barn, but at least that could be rebuilt. What concerned him most was what the fire meant. Someone on the ranch had set that fire intentionally.

Someone close by had just tried to kill them.

SIX

Battling the blaze turned out to be an all-night affair. After she and Miles were both checked out by EMTs and given oxygen, Miles joined his brothers and the local volunteer fire department to contain the fire as best he could with his wrenched shoulder. It wasn't broken but she could see it still hurt him. She wanted to help but all she could do was watch as the flames consumed the barn until the fire was finally extinguished for good.

She and the rest of the family did their best to keep the men fighting the blaze well provisioned with fresh water to drink or coffee and snacks. She overheard Paul telling Miles that he agreed with his assessment of the fire as a deliberate act of arson. He'd found the gas can and the charred remains of the ladder, and determined that was where the fire had started. The loft had been the target and the fire had been intentionally set.

Melissa shuddered as she listened to that conversation. She noticed the way Miles's shoulders tensed and his jaw hammered. This had been another attempt on her life and this one had come close to succeeding. Too close.

Miles rubbed his face and gave a loud sigh before turning back to his brother. She could see his mind working, trying to figure out all the angles. He was probably plotting out their departure from the ranch, figuring out where they could go from here. She didn't want to go. Despite this attempt, she felt safer here than anywhere they'd been since she'd left the home she'd shared with her mother.

Maybe she just felt safer with Miles than with any other marshal.

She had to confess she'd gotten closer to him than she'd planned on. She knew there was no future for them. But as she recalled that kiss they'd shared in the loft and how right it had felt being in his arms, she knew that she didn't want to be anywhere else. If she was the only one involved, maybe she'd try to see what they could work out between them. But she had her son to think about, too. She couldn't risk both of their hearts and happiness on a feeling, no matter how strong it was growing.

"We have to look at who was here on the ranch at the time of the fire," Miles stated and Paul gave him a knowing look.

"You're thinking about the ranch hands, aren't you? They're just kids, Miles. What reason would any one of them have for wanting to hurt you or Melissa?"

"I don't know." He glanced her way and she saw the same question in his expression. It did seem unlikely that high schoolers from Courtland County, Texas, had any connection to Maxwell Shearer. Did that mean someone else had sneaked onto the ranch? That one of Shearer's men had found her? She gulped hard at that possibility. None of the options were good.

Suddenly, she couldn't breathe. She needed to get away from all this talk about killers and arsonists and trying to figure out who was coming after her. All she wanted was normalcy for herself and for Dylan. Thankfully, he was sleeping in Kellyanne's room, blissfully unaware of the turmoil of their current situation.

She folded her arms and headed for the house. She didn't look at him but she felt Miles's eyes on her as she walked inside. She had to do something, anything, to get her mind off the topic they were discussing. He was the expert. Let him figure it out. She needed a breather from it, from all the running and hiding and attacks. She just simply couldn't take it anymore.

The empty kitchen stared at her. She pulled the mop from the cabinet and began mopping the floor. Just something to keep her hands and mind occupied.

Kellyanne entered and watched her, before walking over to her and putting her arms around her. She tried to push her away, but Kellyanne refused and clung tighter. Melissa didn't want this. She didn't want to fall apart in front of this family that had been too good to her. She didn't want to be weak. She had to remain strong for Dylan's sake, but she couldn't, she just couldn't handle it any longer.

She dropped the mop as the tears flowed through her and she cried on Kellyanne's shoulder.

After her tears were gone, she sat down at the table

and put her hands over her face. Kellyanne remained close by, pouring them each a cup of coffee from the pot that she'd made fresh and also shared with the men still working outside.

Melissa sipped from her mug but she wasn't really able to taste it. She was drained, exhausted from all the hustle and fuss. She wanted to crawl into bed and never wake up until this thing was taken care of.

Kellyanne reached over and took her hand. "My brother will make certain nothing happens to you," she told Melissa. "You and Dylan, you make him happy. I've never seen him so happy since he's been here with the two of you."

Her words only brought more tears, because she knew Kellyanne's reassurance was only the result of a lie, a secret that they'd just been too good at keeping and an act they'd been too good at pretending was real. She longed to tell Kellyanne the truth. That Miles's apparent devotion to her was nothing more than his devotion to his job and that her dependency on him was a necessity for the safety of her and her child. Maybe there was an attraction between them, but that was all it was and all it could ever be.

She didn't know how Miles could keep such secrets from the people who loved him. When this was all over, when she was gone, he would have to answer uncomfortable questions. She had no doubt he would cover up her disappearance with more secrets and untruths. And it broke her heart to think this family would never know just how much their care and support had meant to her and Dylan, and how much she'd grown to love this ranch.

Melissa set down her coffee mug and gripped Kellyanne's hand. "If something happens to me—"

"Nothing is going to happen to you," Kellyanne said, cutting her off. "Miles will protect you and my brothers will find the person who is doing this."

She shook her head. "If something does happen, if I have to leave here, I want you to do me a favor and tell your parents and everyone else how thankful I am for all of you, for allowing us to come here and for treating my son and me like family."

Kellyanne squeezed her hand. "You *are* family."

"I'm not really."

"You are now. It doesn't matter how long you and Miles have known one another. You're married now, which makes you a part of this family."

"But if we weren't married…"

Kellyanne withdrew her hand and gave her a worried look. "Something is wrong, isn't it? Is there trouble in the marriage already?"

She shook her head. "No, it's nothing like that."

"Melissa, this person who is after you…is it an old boyfriend? Are you considering going back to him? That would devastate Miles."

"No, Kellyanne. I promise it's not that. It's just—it's just…" She stood up, realizing she couldn't say anything more. "I should go check on Dylan and make sure all this commotion hasn't woken him up. I don't want him to be frightened." She hurried from the room and up the stairs, opening and closing the bedroom door behind her. The fact that she was running from Kellyanne to hide in her bedroom wasn't lost on Melissa.

Dylan was still asleep on the bed. Nothing woke that kid when he was sleeping, and she was thankful again for such a sound sleeper. It was a small thing, but it did make all of this easier. She sat with him, trying to come to some kind of resolution in her mind. She knew getting too close to Miles was a mistake, but she couldn't seem to resist.

She glanced out the window and up into the beautiful sky as morning dawned and found herself praying that God would sort all of this out for her. Was He listening? She didn't feel His hand in all of this, guiding them through it, but He'd sent Miles to her and Dylan, hadn't He? And what would they have done without him? She was certain their outlooks would have been much grimmer with another marshal.

A knock on the door drew her attention away from her prayers. The door opened and Miles poked his head inside. He was covered in dirt and soot, but he'd never looked more handsome to her. "Are you ready to head back to the cabin?"

She nodded and he walked to the bed and picked up Dylan, shuffling him to his uninjured shoulder, then carried him downstairs to the car and buckled him into his car seat. Once they were on the way, he glanced at her. "My sister is worried you're thinking about leaving me for whoever this guy is that's after you."

She wasn't surprised by Kellyanne's overreaction to their conversation, but she *was* surprised Kellyanne had brought it up to him after the night they'd had.

"What else is your family supposed to do but presume the worst when we're constantly keeping secrets from them?" It came out much harsher than she'd intended, but she was tired and frustrated and ready to be free of all the lies.

He sighed and turned his eyes back to the road. "People who know you and trust you shouldn't automatically presume the worst about you."

"I guess that's the problem then, isn't it? They don't know me. And they never will. No one will ever know me, the real me, again, will they? I'll spend my life looking over my shoulder and waiting for the next shoe to drop, never letting anyone close while constantly lying to everyone I'll ever meet."

She hated the way she sounded, so cynical and so unforgiving, but she was feeling sorry for herself. She wanted more out of life than to constantly be living a lie. She wanted to love and trust someone again, but she doubted that would ever happen. The feelings Miles had stirred up in her for love and romance would never lead to anything, with him or with anyone else, because she would always have secrets and no relationship could ever survive based on such lies.

He carried Dylan into the bedroom and placed him on the bed. Melissa pulled off his shoes then covered him up. She stroked his hair as the tears threatened to flow again. This was not the life she wanted for her son and she still didn't know what—or if—she would tell him about this when he was older.

Why, Mama. Why didn't you ever tell me?

She walked into the living room and fell onto the

couch. Miles had cleaned up while she was in with Dylan feeling sorry for herself. He handed her a cup of hot tea and she took it from him and sipped it.

He sat beside her and stroked her hair. "Are you okay?" he asked, and she wasn't sure how to answer.

"I don't know. I'm tired of all of this." She stood and walked to the fireplace. "I don't know how you can live this way—lying all the time, constantly facing danger."

He sidled up behind her and put his arms around her. Despite her misgivings, she didn't protest. She wanted to be in his arms, wanted him to reassure her that everything was going to be okay even if she knew in her heart that it wasn't.

"We will find the mole and we'll stop Shearer. I promise I won't leave you until I know for certain you and Dylan are safe." He'd meant that to be reassuring, she thought to herself, but it only served to remind her that he would be leaving her. She and Dylan would have a new identity and they would have to hide out for the rest of their lives. Miles wouldn't be joining them. She'd never see him again. She moved closer to him and rested her head on his chest, and he wrapped his arms around her.

She only knew one thing for certain.

She didn't want to go.

After cleaning up and getting a few hours of much-needed sleep, Miles joined Paul and Josh by the new bunkhouse. He hated having to do this, and Josh especially didn't like it, but they needed to speak with Luke and the other hands about the fire. He wasn't trying to be accusatory, especially since his brother had told him about other arsons in the area, but he had to make certain none of these kids had been involved and, if they had, he'd need to know if they were working for Shearer or his men.

Josh quickly made introductions. In addition to Luke, whom he'd already met, three other boys lived in the bunkhouse and did chores around the Silver Star— Gavin Myers, Roy Thompson, and Cory Mayfair. Miles had seen them all last night helping to extinguish the fire, but there hadn't been time for introductions then.

Each of them looked hesitant and worried as Paul got right to the point of their visit.

"We believe the fire was intentionally set."

Miles watched their expressions when Paul dropped that bit of news. They all seemed to react appropriately, with shock and surprise and concern.

"By who?" Cory asked.

"We don't know, so we're questioning everyone we know was on the ranch at the time when the fire began."

Roy, who was sitting on the top mattress of a set of bunk beds, addressed his fellow bunkmates. "They think one of us is responsible for the fire."

"That's not true—why would they think that?" Luke jumped to his feet in what felt like an effort to defend Miles and Josh and Paul, but Roy quickly leaped off the top bunk and faced him down.

"Because they believe we're criminals, that's why."

"That's not true. I don't want to believe any one of you are responsible for this," Josh stated. "But we have to ask the questions. Now, where were each of you at the time of the fire?"

Gavin finally spoke up. "We were here, Sheriff. All four of us were here together when we heard the shouting about the fire. That's when we ran out to help."

Miles glanced at each one of them and they all nodded, except Roy, who continued to sulk. "Is that true?" Miles demanded of Roy.

He glanced at Miles, and at first Miles thought the younger man was going to give him another smart-aleck remark. But he didn't. He sighed and nodded his head. "Yeah, that's right. We were all here."

"I'll want to speak to you all individually," Josh stated. "I'll take your statements down at the sheriff's office." They walked out of the bunkhouse and Josh stopped to look at Miles as the boys climbed into his truck and Paul headed into the house.

"Do you believe them?" Miles asked him.

"I have no reason not to. Gavin especially isn't known to lie and I can't believe he would lie to protect someone else. But I'll question them all in depth and if their stories don't match up, we'll know."

He'd believed the boys, too. Their answers had sounded honest, and their shock when they'd learned the fire had been deliberately set had seemed sincere. He recognized himself in Roy Thompson, because of his intensity and anger. The boy struck Miles as a hothead, but he had no reason to want to harm Miles or Melissa, or the Avery family in general, by burning down the barn. Not that Miles knew of, at least.

But if none of the ranch hands were responsible for

the fire, and no one in his family was, either, they were back to the drawing board when it came to identifying the culprit.

Josh stopped before he climbed into his truck and turned back to Miles. "This isn't the first case of arson we've had in the county recently."

Miles nodded. "Paul mentioned that to me. Have you had any leads on those?"

Josh shook his head. "No. So far, we don't have any leads. I'm just happy everyone got out safely."

Miles watched him leave, then turned and looked at the remnants of the barn. It was a total wreck and would need to be rebuilt. Paul had mentioned an arsonist in the area, so that made sense as a reason that had nothing to do with the Shearer case, but it struck him as odd that it had just so happened the fire was set while Melissa was inside the barn.

Someone had tried to kill them, again, and Miles still had no idea who or if their location had been compromised.

The weather turned sunny and mild that afternoon so the men decided to clean up the barn area as best they could, and Miles jumped in to help. Melissa gathered Dylan and a few toys the Averys had found for him to play with and joined everyone outside. Dylan took off running, his little body bursting with energy. She was glad the weather was mild so he could be outside and run off some of that restlessness.

Diane and Kellyanne gathered some boxes and started making up treat bags for the Christmas banquet and Melissa quickly offered her help. She desperately needed the distraction. Miles had assured her that they had found no evidence that Shearer or his men had located them. Other barns in the area had also been set on fire, and Josh suspected a local arsonist was also responsible for last night's incident. But none of that calmed the restless anxiousness that filled her. It seemed like it was only a matter of time before the next attack—one that definitely *would* be aimed at her.

Miles headed toward the porch and Melissa handed him a bottle of water, which he guzzled. He was dressed in jeans and boots and was wearing his cowboy hat. He looked very rustic and rugged, and she couldn't help the appreciation that rushed through her.

"How is it going?"

He shrugged. "It's going to take a long while to clean it up and rebuild, but at least the horses were all rescued. I'm afraid the Woodwards' horses have been traumatized all over again." He turned and looked at Dylan spinning happily and without worry. That was how she always wanted to see him. She didn't want him to have to spend his life constantly anxious and unsure, unable to trust. She hoped Miles could make that happen.

Miles took her hand and smiled down at her. "I think Dylan is having a good time."

She smiled back and leaned into him. "He is. Thank you for this." She was growing to depend on this handsome marshal more and more. In spite of herself, she wanted to lean on him. He didn't appear to mind it. She wished she was free to explore these new feelings that were emerging around Miles. He was a good man. And he loved his family, despite the secrets only she knew he was keeping. It still bothered her that he'd deceive his family, but she understood his reasons. Someone in his marshals service family, people he trusted and considered friends, was likely betraying them by giving out information about her case. She shuddered and Miles must have felt it because he put his arms around her.

"Are you okay?"

She looked up into his eyes and saw genuine concern. She wasn't just another case to him and that meant a lot to her. Did he treat all his WITSEC clients this way? Her face warmed as she recalled their kiss in the barn. Probably not.

"I'm fine. Just bad memories."

He pulled her to him and she soaked in the feel of his strength. She hadn't thought about another man this way since Vick. No one had made her feel so safe and protected before and, now more than ever, it was just what she needed. She was tired of being strong and he seemed to instinctively know and understand that.

His brother called to him and he squeezed her hand. "I'll be right back."

She watched him walk away and felt her face warm at her own thoughts. Brushing them back firmly, she realized she didn't hear Dylan. He was so active that it was never good when he was quiet unless he was sleeping. She turned to look for him. He wasn't in the clearing playing with the toys any longer. She glanced around, but didn't see him. She was filled with worry, but she tried to calm herself, reminding herself not to overreact.

She turned to Mr. and Mrs. Avery and Kellyanne on the porch. "Did one of you take Dylan inside?"

Kellyanne's face showed concern. "I didn't." She looked to her parents. "Did you?"

They both claimed they hadn't seen him.

Panic began to fill Melissa. She hurried toward the barn, where the men were working. If he'd gone in there, he might get injured before anyone realized he was nearby. As it turned out, though, she heard him before she reached the barn.

She turned and spotted him inside the corral with several of the horses she recognized as the Woodwards' horses. Melissa knew next to nothing about horses, but she knew that these had been traumatized twice by fires, and she could easily believe that they might react badly to any sudden, unexpected movement. She wanted to cry out to her son to come back, but no words would come. She ran toward the corral and climbed over the fence, scooping Dylan into her arms just as the wild horse that was closest to him began to buck and neigh loudly. That frightened Dylan and he cried out, screaming in fear at the top of his lungs, which only spooked the horses even more. One of them lunged at them. She tried to move toward the gate, but the horse went crazy and bolted toward them, causing the other horses to do the same.

Fear filled her. They needed to get out of here before they were trampled. She spun around and the horse reared on its hind legs and kicked at her. She screamed before turning around again only to be confronted by another horse bucking at her. She shielded Dylan as best she could as the horse kicked at her, hitting her in the arm and knocking her off her feet. She and Dylan hit the ground as blinding pain raced through her. But she couldn't stop to think about her injury. They had to get out of this pen before the horses trampled them. She scooped up Dylan again with her other arm and tried to find her way out but the dust and horses blocked her way.

They were trapped.

"Melissa, stay calm." Miles's voice reached her from a distance. He sounded so far away but she spotted him and his brother at the fence.

She pulled Dylan toward her, but his cries of fear only continued to spook the horses, who ran around them, sending dust flying and keeping her from seeing any way out. The screeches of the horses seemed to surround her.

Miles and Paul entered the corral and Miles jumped in front of her and Dylan, covering them while Paul tried to calm the horses. She was terrified but thankful that Miles was here now and that she wasn't alone. After pulling her up to her feet, Miles backed her up toward the fence as Paul called out to the horses and tried to rein them in. Once they reached the fence, he grabbed Dylan from her arms and hoisted him over, then reached for her hand.

"I don't think I can climb over," she said, holding her arm, which was throbbing with pain and wouldn't cooperate.

He didn't hesitate. He scooped her up, too, and hoisted her over the fence. His father was waiting to help steady her on the other side. She glanced back for Miles and spotted him hurrying back to help his brother calm the horses. Dylan was still crying but his cries seemed quieter and farther away. He'd had a terrible fright and so had she, and her heart was still pounding at the idea that Miles could be hurt. She turned around and spotted Kellyanne carrying Dylan away from the pen. Good. She could take him back to the house, where his cries wouldn't continue to spook the horses, but Melissa needed to get to him to comfort him. She moved to go to him, but pain rushed through her and her knees buckled as she collapsed. John grabbed her before she fell.

"Sit down," he instructed, lowering her to the ground. "You're going to be fine."

"Dylan."

"Kellyanne has him. He's safe now." He checked her over and she flinched when he touched her arm. "Looks like you might have a broken arm. We need to get you to the hospital."

"Miles." She grunted out his name between gasps of pain.

His father did his best to keep her calm. "He's fine. He's helping Paul and the boys calm the horses. You and Dylan are very fortunate. Horses don't usually like to step on anyone, but these are easily spooked. They could have really hurt you both."

Somehow, she'd sensed that those horses were out of control and dangerous. How had Dylan gotten into that pen in the first place? She should have been watching him more closely. She should ask John to take her to

Dylan, but she didn't want to leave without first knowing that Miles was safe, too.

The yelling and noise from the pen grew fainter and she looked up to see Miles approaching her. He was covered in dirt from head to toe, but he shook it off. He looked to be okay. She couldn't stop herself. She fell into his arms as tears flowed. He held her tighter than he would have if she was merely a client, surely. Something had changed between them. She knew it then. She felt it. This wasn't the embrace of two people who barely knew one another. She'd been frightened for his life and it had nothing to do with him being a marshal and her being a witness in his custody.

She heard his heart hammering against his chest and his heavy breathing. She looked up into his eyes and touched his face.

He kissed her hand and nodded his head. "I'm okay. Are you...?"

She quickly reassured him. "We're okay, too... thanks to you."

"Not so okay," his father corrected and only then did she realize that she was still in Miles's arms and his family thought nothing of it. But, of course, they didn't think anything of it. Because of the secret. Because they believed a lie that she and Miles were married and in love. "I think her arm is broken. She needs to go to the hospital. Dylan seems to be unharmed but we should have him checked out, too, just in case. How did this happen?"

Miles looked to her for an answer and she rushed to find her words. "I—I'm not sure. I realized that

I couldn't hear Dylan playing anymore, and when I looked around, I couldn't find him. When I went to go search for him, I spotted him inside the horse corral. He started crying and the horses went wild."

John nodded. "He spooked them. Those Woodward mares spook easily."

"I don't know what he was doing there or how he got in." She felt her face flush this time for an entirely different reason. "I should have been watching him more closely."

"We all should have," Miles stated. "He's a child who doesn't understand the dangers of horses."

"I'm not so sure," Paul said as he approached them. "How could he have gotten inside that pen without anyone noticing? The wire fencing around the wood means he couldn't crawl through the slats and the gate was securely locked when I checked it twenty minutes ago— not that I think he could have opened it on his own, anyway. He would have had to climb over the fence and that wouldn't have been easy for someone his size."

Melissa glanced at the fence and remembered the difficult time she'd had getting over it and she was much taller than Dylan. She glanced at her hands, which were bleeding from the wire. Dylan had none of those injuries and he wasn't a climber. Paul was right. How had he gotten into that pen without anyone noticing?

She looked at Miles, whose face paled as he reached the same conclusion. It wouldn't have been easy for Dylan to get inside. Someone had to have helped him… and left him there. Anger burst through her. Someone had intentionally put her child in danger's path.

Miles pulled her to him and accidently touched her arm, causing her to wince in pain. "We'll figure this out later. We need to get her to the hospital. Can you walk to the car?"

"I think so." She wanted to say *yes* more firmly and confidently, wanted to be strong in front of him, but the pain was blinding. She leaned on him as they headed for the SUV. At one point, he was nearly carrying her, but she made it to the car and Miles helped her buckle in.

She spotted Kellyanne rush from the house with Dylan in her arms. His face was tear-streaked and red, but he seemed to be okay.

"I don't think he was hurt," Kellyanne assured her. "Only frightened. I tried to ask him how he got inside that pen but he couldn't tell me."

She thanked Kellyanne and reassured Dylan that everything was going to be okay. Kellyanne buckled Dylan into his car seat then crawled into the back seat. But as Miles put the car into gear and headed for the hospital, between a moment of overwhelming pain, Melissa couldn't help wondering again how Dylan had gotten into that pen and what would have happened to both of them if Miles hadn't intervened in time.

He'd saved them…for now. But if someone had intentionally tried to harm Dylan, and probably her, too, that meant they'd been here, close enough to grab him without her noticing, close enough to get to them while they were standing by the barn. Someone who was specifically targeting her—not an arsonist who was local to the area, or hunters who'd accidentally fired in the wrong direction. This attack had been deliberate and unmistakable.

And it meant they were no longer safe even at the ranch.

The bad guys had found them again.

SEVEN

The doctor X-rayed Melissa's arm and confirmed a small break. He gave her something for pain, then told her that she would be fine before saying someone would come in to put a cast on it shortly. Miles was thankful the injury hadn't been more serious. He knew it could have been much worse.

His parents appeared in the emergency room and assured them both that Dylan was fine. "The doctor gave him a complete examination. He wasn't hurt at all."

He saw Melissa's relief at that news. She'd been edgy and unable to relax since the moment they'd been taken into separate treatment rooms because she hadn't had Dylan in her sight. It had taken all his assurances to convince her that the boy was safe with his parents. Moments later, Kellyanne and their parents arrived with Dylan, who rushed over to the hospital bed. Miles lifted him up so Melissa could hug him and he saw a peace wash over her. Despite her own injuries, her son's well-being was of utmost importance to her. She was a good mom and he admired how much she loved this little boy. In fact, Miles had grown quite fond of him, too.

"We thought we would take Dylan back home with us," his dad stated. "He's already getting restless and it looks as though you all are going to be a while getting that cast."

Melissa face twisted with worry, but Kellyanne rushed to tamp down her concern. "We'll take excellent care of him. That's a promise."

Although he could see Melissa didn't want to let him out of her sight, she finally agreed. It was what was best for Dylan. A hospital was no place for a three-year-old—especially one who had had a scare and could use some comfort. He handed his sister an extra key to the SUV so she could get Dylan's car seat out and they left.

Miles pulled up a chair and sat beside Melissa as the doctor came in and placed a cast on her arm. He held her hand through the procedure and tried to insist that everything was going to be okay, yet he could see her mind working, processing what had happened.

She clutched his hand with her good one and fear settled on her face. "Are we safe here?"

"Of course, you're safe. Don't jump to conclusions," Miles warned her. He wasn't ready to say this was a deliberate attack. True, it shouldn't have been easy for Dylan to climb into that pen, but he'd seen kids do things that no one would have thought they could before.

Dylan was three years old and in awe of the ranch and the horses. It was still possible he'd climbed in there on his own and this was nothing more than an accidental incident.

But the fear in Melissa's face was real. She believed they were no longer safe here. He refused to accept that yet. This was his home. He didn't want to consider that someone had sneaked onto the ranch and managed to get to them. He couldn't make his brain process that possibility.

The pain meds finally kicked in and Melissa began to relax as they waited for her to be discharged. Before he knew it, she was sleeping. But he couldn't. His senses were on high alert, ready to confront any danger that might come their way.

Josh entered the room, spotted Melissa sleeping and motioned for Miles to join him in the hallway. He saw Paul and their father were with him.

"Dad called and told me what happened. I'm sorry it took so long for me to get here. How is Melissa?"

Miles took a deep breath and tried to settle his nerves. "She broke her arm and she's pretty shaken up, but otherwise, she's okay."

Paul massaged his own arm, which had gotten strained from wrestling to settle the horses. "She was fortunate it was no worse than that."

He hated that his brother had been injured, but he was glad Paul had been there. He wasn't sure he and his dad could have handled them alone. Josh had been at the sheriff's office and Lawson hadn't yet returned from his trip. True, he still had the young group of ranch hands who had rushed in to help, but Miles trusted no one as much as his brothers.

Finally, Josh asked the question everyone had been thinking. "So was this an accident?"

Miles glanced at Paul. He wanted his brother to assure him it had been, but Paul wasn't able to do that. "It's unlikely," he said. "I locked up that pen myself and when I got to it, it was still latched."

Miles couldn't argue that point. "Melissa said she climbed over the fence and she has the marks on her hands to prove it. She didn't enter through the gate and I don't see how Dylan could have unlocked it on his own."

His dad agreed. "I don't think he could. The latch was too high for him."

Josh grimaced and pulled out his notebook. "Okay, then the question is who was there who could have done this?"

Paul answered. "Just the family, plus the ranch hands. They would have no reason to hurt Dylan or Melissa. Also, the vet was there earlier, checking on the pregnant mare, but his truck was gone by the time I thought to look for it."

His dad shook his head. "Dr. Fulton? We've known him for years. He wouldn't harm anyone."

"It wasn't Dr. Fulton. The Woodwards hired a new vet, Dr. Randy Singer. I didn't know him but he seemed okay. You think he might have something to do with the guy who's after Melissa?"

His father looked confused. "Someone is after Melissa?"

"No," Miles stated. "I didn't say that. There is something going on with her that I haven't shared with you all, but I hope you'll trust me enough not to push the matter."

"If you're worried about keeping her safe, the Silver Star is the best place you could have come," his father told him.

"I know. That's why we're here."

"So there is something," his father said.

Miles pulled a hand through his hair and nodded. He wasn't going to be able to keep this secret from his family much longer. "I don't see how anyone could have known our location. It doesn't make any sense. No one should know we are here, which means Melissa shouldn't be targeted."

His father turned to Josh. "Just in case, I'd check out that new vet. If someone was involved, he was the only one on the property that we don't know."

Miles scrubbed a hand over his jaw. This was getting out of control. He still didn't want to admit this had been a planned attack against Melissa and Dylan. Something about this incident didn't sit right with him. If this had been the work of Shearer's men, why all the drawn-out drama of luring or placing Dylan in that pen? Why not just start shooting and take them both out? This didn't seem like the tactic of a trained assassin like Richard Kirby, or a mob boss like Max Shearer. But his brother was right. The latch on that gate was high. Too high for Dylan to have opened it himself. And if it had been opened, a three-year-old certainly wouldn't have closed and latched the gate behind him. Someone had either lured him into that pen, or placed him there and then closed the gate behind them. Hopefully, Dylan would be able to tell them what happened once he calmed down, but it wouldn't hurt to have this Dr. Singer checked out. "Do you have his contact info?" Josh asked Paul.

"He gave me his card the first day he arrived. It's back at the Silver Star, but I believe his offices were on the south end of town right at the county line."

"I'll issue a BOLO for him. If any of my deputies see him, they'll let me know. I'll also have Cecile pick up the boys and question them again. I can't imagine that any of them are involved, but if they were on the property, I want to know for certain that this wasn't them."

"Thanks, Josh." Miles hated to think that the very kids his brothers were mentoring had a hand in trying to harm Melissa or Dylan, and he couldn't think of one reason why they would. But he couldn't discount the fact that they'd been there on the property both times when she'd come close to dying and that they would have had the opportunity to grab Dylan and place him inside that pen. Dylan might not have even cried out if one of them approached him because he'd seen them before.

All he wanted to know was if whoever had done this was somehow connected to Shearer and if his men had somehow found Melissa.

Miles's father took the moment to place his hand on his shoulder. "Don't you worry, son. We'll look after Melissa. No one is going to harm her while she's at the Silver Star."

He should have been annoyed at his family's insistence on butting into his business, but he wasn't.

His dad's words comforted him and gave him the reassurance he needed that he'd made the right choice in
bringing her here. Anyone of his family, including his
mother and sister, would protect Melissa and Dylan
from any attacks with a fierce determination no bad
guy had ever seen before.

But his train of thought brought him back to the
same place. What connection would a group of teen-
age delinquents or a country veterinarian have with a
mob boss or a paid assassin?

Miles helped Melissa into the car. She was still
groggy from the pain meds, but they seemed to be helping to make her more comfortable. He assisted buck-
ling her into her seat and she gave him a soft smile. He
smoothed back her hair. He knew she was anxious to
get back to the house to check on Dylan. Whether or not
it had been an attack, it had shaken him and made him
realize that he'd become too distracted by this lovely
brunette and her son to be able to do his job properly.
He had to back away, distance himself from her, but
that was going to be difficult to do when his family believed that he was married to her.

He started the SUV and headed to the Silver Star.
Night had fallen and the road they were on was nearly
deserted. Melissa dozed in the seat beside him while he
worked on filtering the day's events through his brain.

Headlights in his rearview mirror caught his eye
and he glanced behind him. A car was approaching
quickly. Its headlights were on bright and it wasn't slowing down. He gripped the steering wheel and glanced

over to see Melissa was still dozing. His senses went on alert, but he reminded himself not to overreact. It was probably nothing. Probably just kids out for a joyride.

Miles stepped off the accelerator to slow the SUV so the other driver could pass them, but the driver didn't seem to take the hint.

"What's happening?" Melissa asked, raising her head from the seat and rubbing sleep from her eyes.

"Someone's behind us and they're not going around."

She glanced back and her face paled. "Is it them?"

His gut was telling him it was but he didn't want to jump to conclusions. "It's more likely that it's just some kids messing with us."

He sped up and the car sped up, too, finally swerving to pass them, but as the car came closer, he had a bad feeling.

"Hang on," he shouted at Melissa as he floored the accelerator and took off. The car followed suit.

Melissa's voice was frantic as she shouted out details of what they were doing. "The passenger window is coming down and the passenger is leaning out. Miles, he has a gun."

"Brace yourself," Miles shouted as gunfire filled the air. A bullet blasted through the back window.

"Get down."

Melissa crouched down as much as she could as Miles did his best to keep the car out of firing range. He swerved in front of the car and tried to run them off the road while the other car continued speeding up. The passenger leaned out again and fired another round of blasts and he heard the ding of the bullets hitting metal.

They had to get away from this car before the shooter managed to hit one of the tires or, worse, one of them.

He grabbed the phone from its cradle on the dash and handed it to Melissa. "Call Josh or Paul or whoever you can find. Tell them we're on Boyce Cannon Road and need help."

He glanced into the side mirror and caught a good look at the shooter just as he leaned out of the window of the car and fired, causing the side mirror to fly off the car. Whoever this guy was, he wasn't a great shot.

This blitz attack made no sense to him. Why not target them while they were getting in or out of the car, rather than while they were driving down the road? High-speed targets were a lot harder to hit, especially if you weren't a skilled shooter. Maybe they wanted it to look like an accident, but that would be difficult to do given all the bullet holes.

The driver sped up again and the shooter fired but the shots missed. Something didn't seem right about all of this, but one thing was for certain…

They'd definitely been found by someone who wanted them dead.

The shooter fired again and the bullet whizzed past Miles's head and slammed through the windshield. Miles jerked the steering wheel instinctively and lost control of the car. Melissa screamed as they smashed into a tree. Miles's head slammed against the steering wheel and blinding pain shot through him as they jerked to a stop. He tried to open his eyes and reach for his weapon, but his vision was blurry and he couldn't reach his gun. Melissa was beside him, but she'd stopped screaming. He turned his head and saw her head lowered. She was unconscious. He glanced through the shattered windshield and spotted the bright red of brake lights as their attackers stopped then turned around. And he heard the sound of muffled yelling from his brother through his cell phone, but he couldn't respond as darkness pulled him away.

Melissa's head was pounding when she opened her eyes. At first her vision was blurry, but as she tried to focus she realized what was wrong. They'd crashed the car. She tried to turn her head and saw Miles leaning against the steering wheel. He was unconscious and blood was oozing down his face from a gash on his forehead, but at least he was still breathing. She unbuckled and leaned over to try to wake him. She took a moment to be thankful Dylan hadn't been with them.

But what had happened? Why had Miles become so distracted? Then she remembered. Someone had been following them. Someone had shot at them and Miles had lost control of the car.

Alertness flooded her and she turned to look out the windows. A car was stopped several feet away, only the headlights visible in the darkness. What were they doing? Waiting to see if they'd survived the crash?

She shook Miles's shoulder and called his name. The last thing she remembered was being on the phone with Paul. She couldn't recall what she'd said to him—if he knew where they were and what was going on. She glanced around and found the phone on the floorboard.

Miles began to groan and move. She shook his shoulder again. "Miles, wake up. Wake up! We're in trouble."

But he didn't wake up, not completely. His eyes fluttered but didn't open. She didn't know what to do so she grabbed the phone again and dialed Paul's number. He picked up quickly.

"Paul, you have to help us. We're in trouble."

"Melissa? What happened?"

"Someone was shooting at us. We crashed. Miles is unconscious. I think the person is still out there. I see a car that's just sitting."

"I'm already in my truck. Tell me where you are."

"I don't know. We were heading back to the ranch from the hospital. I don't know the names of the roads." Then she recalled the name Miles had mentioned. "I think Miles said we were on Boyce Cannon Road."

"Hang on. I'm minutes away. Stay on the line with me."

She felt better having a connection and knowing someone was coming to help, but it didn't ease her fears when a car approached. At first, she hoped it was Paul, but it was too soon, and surely he would have said something. She glanced out the window and spotted a car slowing down. Someone trying to help them? She didn't know. She got out and walked around the side of the car.

"What's happening?" Paul's voice asked her.

"Someone's here. Another car just pulled up and stopped a few hundred feet away. Is it you?"

"No, it's not. What are they doing? It's probably someone stopping to help."

She walked toward the car and the door opened, but when the man exited the car, she spotted a gun in his hand. He raised it and fired.

Melissa screamed, dropped the phone and ran back toward the SUV, hiding behind the vehicle as the man approached. The clomping of his boots against the asphalt made an eerie sound. She needed Miles to wake up now. Why hadn't she grabbed his gun? Paul's voice was still yelling at her, but then the man stepped on and crushed the phone, ending the call.

"What do you want?" Melissa screamed. "Why are you doing this?"

No response. She glanced around and saw him approaching from the left, so she moved the other way, sliding around the SUV to the driver's-side window. Looking inside, she saw Miles was still unconscious. She shook his shoulder again, trying to wake him. He groaned and the man turned and headed toward her. She tried to grab the gun at Miles's side holster but the way he was hunched over, she couldn't reach it. Maybe that was for the best—it wasn't like she knew much about how to use it. All she could do was hope that Paul would arrive before this man reached her.

She moved away from the vehicle and slid to the ground, wiggling beneath the SUV. He would find her and there was nowhere to run. She would never make it to the woods before he shot her, and besides, she couldn't leave Miles alone. He would kill him for sure.

It's you he's after, not Miles, she reminded herself. Maybe he would be safer if she ran.

God, please let Paul arrive soon.

She saw the man's boots as he walked around the SUV and she willed her heart to stop hammering against her chest before he heard it. It was so loud. She couldn't breathe, the fear was pressing on her so hard.

He stopped at the driver's door and was probably checking Miles to see if he was breathing. He was going to find her! He had to know she had nowhere to run.

Suddenly, the door jerked open, knocking the man to the ground. Miles jumped on top of him and wrestled for the gun in his hand. The man kicked at Miles and tossed him backward, away from him. He started to raise the gun when a pair of headlights shone from around the corner and blinded him. He swore and ran back toward the car, hopping inside. Both cars roared away as Paul's truck screeched to a stop and he jumped out.

Melissa crawled out from under the SUV and rushed to Miles, who was conscious but still bleeding.

"Are you both all right?" Paul asked.

Miles nodded but grunted. "I'm fine." He glanced at Melissa and concern rocked his expression. "Are you?"

She nodded quickly to alleviate his fears. "I'm okay." Either the painkillers she'd taken for her broken arm were still working or else the adrenaline rushing through her was dulling the pain.

Paul pulled out his phone and made a call, grunting in frustration when it went to voice mail. "Josh isn't answering."

"Try Cecile," Miles suggested. "She'll know where he is."

He made the call and alerted Cecile to the situation, then called for an ambulance.

"I don't need an ambulance," Miles insisted, ordering him to end that call. "I'm fine."

"You hit your head," Melissa responded. "You lost consciousness and were out for a couple of minutes, at least. You should get checked out."

He pushed to his feet, using the SUV for support. "I said I'm fine." He walked toward Paul's truck and opened the door, sliding inside.

Melissa glanced at Paul, who nodded for her to follow him. "He's probably just beating himself up that he got knocked out when you needed him."

She crawled in beside Miles while Paul remained outside, obviously to give them some privacy. She placed a comforting hand on his arm. "Are you sure you're okay?"

"I'm fine." He pulled off his button-up shirt, wadded it up and pressed it against his forehead where the gash was bleeding. Blood already stained his T-shirt.

"I was scared. I thought he was going to kill us both."

"I'm sorry he got the jump on me. That shouldn't have happened."

"It's not your fault. I understand that things happen."

"Things don't just happen, Melissa. They can't. It's my job to make sure they don't. You don't seem to get that. When things just happen, people die. People I'm supposed to protect. I failed you today."

She touched his arm again and leaned her head against his shoulder. "I don't feel like you failed me. I'm still here. I'm safe."

"You're not safe. They know where you are. Don't you see? You've been compromised. I can't deny it any longer." He rapped his hand against the dashboard. "I was a fool to believe you were ever really safe."

"You were trying to do the right thing. I understand that. I'm glad you brought us here. Dylan and I have needed this break."

"Yeah, well, break is over. It's time to get you somewhere safe."

Paul climbed into the truck and started the engine. "I'm taking you to the ER. You at least need to have that gash stitched up."

Miles started to protest only to have his brother give him a don't-mess-with-me look. Finally, Miles nodded his agreement. "Fine, but I'm not staying overnight."

He grabbed Melissa's hand and clung to it and she seemed to understand his concern. He wasn't going to leave her side again, even for medical attention. He was going to stay with her until this was finished. It didn't matter that it hadn't been his choice to be knocked out.

"Dylan!"

Miles grabbed Paul's phone. If Shearer's men knew to find them on the road to the hospital, then they knew about the Silver Star, too. They could go after her son. "Who's at the ranch?"

"Just Mom and Dad when I left. They were watching Dylan."

Miles pressed the icon to call, and his dad answered. "Has anyone been there? Have you seen anything? A strange car? Someone sneaking around?"

"No, why?"

"Where are you?"

"We're inside the house."

"Good. Stay there. Lock the doors and grab one of the rifles."

"What's happening?"

"Someone just ran me and Melissa off the road and tried to kill us. We're concerned he might try to go after Dylan next."

He heard his dad's voice turn to hardened determination. "Well, he'll have to get through us first. Are you both okay?"

"We're fine. Paul is taking me to the ER to get a wound stitched up, but we're good. Have you spoken to Josh? We can't get him on the phone."

"I haven't. I'll keep trying to call him."

He ended the call and handed the phone back to his brother, then slid his arm around Melissa and pulled her close to him. Fear was reverberating off her, but the scent of her berry-scented shampoo sent his senses reeling. He'd nearly lost her, nearly cost her her life. He had to do better for her and Dylan. He'd never lost a witness and he wouldn't start with her. It wasn't just his professional pride. This case mattered more to him than anything had before. And that was why he needed to be at his very best. He'd gotten too close to her for his own good. He'd been too unguarded. That's why this guy had been able to ambush them without him seeing it coming. It had been a rookie mistake that nearly cost them both their lives. It couldn't happen again.

With the way she melted into his arms, he knew

keeping his professional distance wasn't going to be easy. But his heart wasn't what was important. Keeping her safe and alive was priority number one. Any foolish dreams he had about a life with her and Dylan didn't—couldn't—matter. They were impossible dreams, anyway. She would always be in danger and he could never be with her while she was. He would have to leave his job as a marshal and enter WITSEC with her and he didn't think he could ever give up being a marshal.

Josh arrived at the ER while a doctor was stitching up Miles's head. "What happened?"

"Someone was firing at us. He hit the windshield, and my hand jerked on the steering wheel until I drove us into a tree."

"Did you get a description of the guy or of the car? Did you recognize the shooter?"

Miles shook his head. "Not a great description of the guy. The car was a silver sedan. I couldn't really tell make and model and I didn't see the license plate."

"There was another car, too," Melissa told them. "It arrived after we'd crashed. A man got out and tried to shoot us."

"Did you get a look at him?"

She shook her head and Miles sighed. Despite wrestling with the man, he couldn't identify him, either. "Honestly, they were on top of us before I knew what happened." He glanced over at Melissa. It was because of his attraction to her that he hadn't been paying attention.

No more.

Josh turned to look at her, then nodded. "I'll get a

BOLO out for the cars and I've got deputies already at the scene. They can canvass the area. Maybe some-one saw one of these cars and got a better look at the shooter."

"Doubtful. There aren't many houses out that way and the ones that are are set far off the road. Unless someone happened to be driving by, I doubt they saw anything."

"Where were you?" Paul asked Josh. "Melissa tried to call you and so did I. It went straight to voice mail."

"I was busy. I came as soon as I received Cecile's message."

Miles shot a look at Paul. Josh was acting odd and he looked nervous. It was unusual for him not to answer his phone, but he had to give his brother the benefit of the doubt. He was human and being tied up wasn't a crime. He couldn't be at everyone's beck and call 24 hours a day. That's why he had a crew of deputies.

Josh gave him a grim look. "Maybe it's time you told us all what's really going on. Why is someone after Melissa?" He turned to look at her. "Why does someone want you dead? Is this a jealous ex-boyfriend or something?"

She folded her arms as best she could with the cast, but shook her head. "I wish it were that simple."

Josh turned to Miles. "I can't keep either of you safe if I don't know what's going on. You need to trust us, Miles. We're your family."

He glanced at Melissa and saw acceptance in her face. She didn't like the secrets, anyway, but had kept silent because he'd asked her to. But now even he had to admit that his brothers were right. He couldn't keep her protected alone, at least not here. Their location had most definitely been compromised. His mind was spinning, trying to figure out how they'd been found, because if Shearer's men could find them here, they weren't safe anywhere. He needed his brothers, needed their help to keep her safe while they remained at the ranch, which wouldn't be for long—they had to know the truth.

He waited for the doctor to finish up and walk out. He glanced at each of them. Knowing would change everything. It would change the way they saw him and it might even place their lives in danger in the future. Plus, he'd kept this secret from them for so long. Would they be angry at him? Would they be able to forgive him for his deception?

Thinking of the possible consequences made him feel sick to his stomach, but he refused to go back on his decision. All that mattered to him now was keeping Melissa safe. Bringing his brothers into the secret was the safest thing for her right now. He had to risk it.

"The truth?" Miles asked.

Paul nodded and folded his arms, readying himself. "The truth. What's going on? Who is after Melissa?"

He took a deep breath. "The man after Melissa is a very dangerous contract killer named Richard Kirby. He works for a mob boss named Maxwell Shearer."

They both stared at him, then at Melissa, then back at him. "How on earth did she get mixed up with a mob boss?" Josh asked.

"Accidentally. Twenty years ago, Melissa's mother

worked for Shearer. She uncovered some fraudulent activity in his accounts and went to the authorities. She testified against him and was the key witness in convicting him. Then, a few months ago, an appeals court overturned his conviction and sent his case back to the lower courts to be retried. Four weeks ago, Shearer hired Kirby to find and murder Melissa's mother in order to prevent her from testifying against him again. Melissa walked in on her mother's murder—just in time to clearly see the killer. Fortunately, she managed to escape the house and ran for help."

"Only now she's the witness because she saw his face," Paul stated.

Miles nodded. "She identified the shooter through his mug shot."

Josh rubbed a hand over his face. "You should have told us this earlier, Miles."

He glanced at Melissa with a silent question. Should he finish the story? Tell them everything and let the pieces fall where they may? She nodded to silently encourage him on.

"I don't understand," Paul said. "How did they find her? Why wasn't she in protective custody or witness protection?"

His brother had just landed on the exact question to ask to reveal the rest of the secret. "She was. Melissa and her mother entered the witness protection program twenty years ago. Melissa was only five years old at the time. She had no idea she was even in the program until the marshals arrived after her mother was killed. She's been under the marshals' protection ever since."

They both turned to look at him, understanding dawning in their expressions. Miles continued. "Melissa isn't my wife. She's my witness—and it's my sworn duty to protect her."

EIGHT

He saw his brothers processing this new information. Shock was written across their faces.

Paul folded his arms and took a long, deep breath. "I can't believe you didn't tell us."

Josh nodded. "Guess we should have been more suspicious when you brought her home out of the blue."

"Wait, what do you mean, she's not your wife?" They all turned to find Kellyanne standing in the doorway. She'd overheard their conversation.

"What are you doing here?" Miles demanded.

"Mom called and told me you and Melissa were in a car accident. I was making sure you were both okay." She walked in and looked at Melissa in the corner. "Is this true? You're not married to my brother?"

She glanced at Miles, then gave a nod as her answer to Kellyanne's question. He could see how this was tearing her up. She'd never wanted to hurt this family or lie to them, but anyone could see the hurt and anger in Kellyanne's face. Melissa had grown to really like Miles's sister and Miles knew that the feeling had been mutual. They'd become close, like sisters, but they weren't sisters and they never would be.

Kellyanne turned to Miles. "You lied to us."

He stiffened, then stood to face her. "I had a job to do. I couldn't tell you."

Josh regained his bearings. "Back to this guy who is after Melissa. How do you think he found out she's here? And why is she here instead of in a real safe house?"

"That's another thing I should tell you. I brought Melissa here because no one in the marshals service could know where she was. We believe there's a leak in the WITSEC agency."

"A leak? Who would do that?"

"I don't know, and so far my boss hasn't made any headway in finding out. All I know is that these men who are after Melissa keep finding her. Four weeks ago, right after she was placed in protective custody, she was ambushed. The marshals on duty were able to get her to safety, but two of them were killed in the attack. They moved her to another location. Two days later, the marshals assigned to her learned of an impending threat and moved her again. After that, it took Shearer's men five days to find them, but they did. My boss gave me this assignment with explicit instructions to tell no one where we were. Not even he knows. The rest of the office doesn't even realize I'm on this case—they think Dad had a relapse and I came home to help. So how did they find us?"

Paul folded his arms across his chest. "It doesn't matter how they discovered it. They just did."

"It matters to me. I have no idea who I can and can't trust in my own agency. A WITSEC inspector who is giving up witnesses is a major breach. It can't be ignored, but my first priority has to be to Melissa and Dylan."

Kellyanne gasped. "Dylan! That's why you asked about him and told Dad to get the rifle. You thought someone was coming after him."

"After the crash, I wanted to make sure he was safe. I didn't know where that guy who ran us off the road was going."

Melissa stood and addressed Kellyanne. "Is Dylan still with your parents?"

"He's still at the ranch with Mom and Dad. Don't worry. They'll keep him safe." She looked at Miles and her expression hardened again. "Learning he's not their grandchild might kill them however."

He didn't care for her jab at the moment. "I'm sorry, Kellyanne. Really, I am, but I can't think about that now. I did what I thought was best. Can we please just deal with this for now? We'll figure that out later."

She gave a regretful nod. "What do you want me to do?"

"Take us back to the ranch. We need to pack up and get out of town before these guys have another opportunity to take us out."

Paul stopped him. "You can't go."

"I can't stay. Her life is in danger. I can't risk staying now that this location is known."

"You just said yourself that you don't have anyone you can trust. Well, you know you can trust us. Stay here and let us be your backup. Now that we are aware of what she's involved in, we can help you keep her safe."

"I can't ask you to do that."

Josh stepped forward. "You don't have to ask. We're here for you, Miles. We always have been. Besides, we know these men are in town. You've got law enforcement on your side. That's an advantage you won't have anywhere else. This is the perfect opportunity to capture them and make sure she stays safe."

Paul and Kellyanne both agreed, but Miles ran a hand through his hair. "No, I'm sorry. I have to get her somewhere else. I appreciate your willingness to help, but capturing this madman isn't my job. Keeping Melissa and Dylan safe is."

"But wouldn't it be better if we could do both? You keep her safe and we'll do the legwork to try to find this guy who's after her. If he's in town, someone must know something."

Still, Miles hesitated. He turned to Melissa, his eyes questioning. He could see she wanted to say yes, to accept his family's help. And he wanted that, too.

He looked back to his family. "Can you give us a moment alone to talk about it?"

They all agreed and stepped out of the room.

Miles turned to her. "Well? What do you think? I say it's too dangerous. We need to leave."

"I'll never be able to rest easy if we don't capture this guy," she told him. "Dylan and I will always be running. That's not the kind of life I want for my son." Or for herself, if she was honest. She wanted a family just like the one Miles had shown her. A family that stood together and helped one another out, who faced danger and trouble together, united. She'd grown used to this clan and would miss them when she left here, but if they could help her stay safe a little while longer, then why run? "Besides, you said you trusted your family."

"I do trust them. With my life, not with yours and Dylan's. That's a responsibility I trust to no one but myself."

"I don't want to leave," she whispered. She reached up and touched his face, running her fingers over his jaw. She wasn't ready to say goodbye to the Averys, but mostly she wasn't ready to say goodbye to Miles. "I haven't felt as safe anywhere else as I have here and that's even with the attacks against me."

He pulled her into an embrace and hugged her, pulling her so tight against him that, for a moment, she couldn't breathe. "I shouldn't do this," he whispered. "I shouldn't be putting your lives at risk this way."

She broke their embrace and locked eyes with him. "If we leave the Silver Star and they find us again, we'll have to face them alone. At least here, we have people who can help us. I'm ready for this to be over, Miles. One way or another, I want it to end."

He sighed, then walked to the door and opened it, addressing his brothers and sister. "Looks like we're staying."

By the time the sun rose, Kellyanne had helped Melissa pack her and Dylan's things and transfer them to her bedroom in the main house after Miles determined that it was safer for them to stay there instead of the cabin. It didn't take long because they didn't have much, but Melissa was grateful for the help, and glad to know that Kellyanne wasn't holding a grudge over her secret about being married to Miles.

But Kellyanne did seem sad as she helped them get set up in her room. "What's going on with you?" Melissa asked when she had the opportunity.

Kellyanne sat on the bed and sighed. "I thought I had another sister. It's been me against the boys for all of my life. When Lawson married Bree, I thought, this is great. I finally have a sister, so I'm not so outnumbered. And when you and Miles arrived at the ranch, I thought I'd gotten another."

Melissa sat beside her and reached for her hand. "That's nice. You were so kind to me. I hated keeping that terrible secret from everyone. It made me feel so guilty, especially when you all were so welcoming."

"I understand why you felt you had to. You trusted Miles and he was just doing his best to keep you safe. At first, I was angry with him for getting married and not telling us. Then I was just happy for him, you know. I was happy that he finally found what he was looking for."

"You're all so close. I'm not used to that."

"Aren't you close to your family?"

"I never really had any. Only my mom. I was an only child, just like my parents." Melissa paused for a moment as she thought about it. "I don't even know if that's true. Mom told me that my dad died before I was born, but maybe he's alive, but wouldn't go into

WITSEC with us." She shrugged it off. "If he's alive, or if I have any aunts or uncles or cousins connected to him or my mom, then I never knew about them. It was always me and my mom. Even my late husband, Vick, didn't have any family. Now, Dylan is all I have."

"He's a precious little boy."

"Thank you. He's enjoyed being here so much. The last several places we've stayed have been hotels or apartments with no room for him to run and jump and play." She felt tears pressing against her face and she covered her mouth to keep them at bay. Kellyanne saw her distress and slid across the bed, putting her arm around Melissa's shoulders.

"It's okay. I guess you've been through a lot, haven't you?"

She nodded. "I try not to focus on it. I do my best to be strong for Dylan's sake, but it's been so hard. And the other marshals who I've dealt with, well, they've been nothing like Miles. They all treated me like I was a criminal." She remembered the marshal who'd let her keep her mother's necklace and realized that wasn't entirely true. "Well, most of them did. But Miles was different from the start. He seemed to care, wanted to make us comfortable. I knew right away he was a good person."

Kellyanne nodded. "He's a great guy. And I think he'll make a great husband one day." She stood and went back to folding clothes. "I still have a hard time believing you two aren't married. You seemed so perfect for one another. And I know Miles has become attached to that kid of yours."

And Dylan was just as attached to him. It was too easy to imagine what a good father Miles would be to Dylan. And what a good husband he'd be. Melissa recalled the way he'd held her and rocked her in his arms, assuring her everything was going to be okay. He'd been the only comfort she'd had since this nightmare started and her growing attraction to him was only making her confusion more pronounced.

She glanced at Kellyanne and felt her face redden with embarrassment. Kellyanne had the strange ability to look right through her and see the feelings she was trying so hard to keep hidden.

Her face broke into a big grin. "I knew it! I knew you weren't that good of actors. You do like him, don't you? You're in love with my brother."

She flushed and was quick to correct her. "It's way too early to claim to be in love with anyone. I've only known your brother a short time."

"But you like him, don't you?"

She couldn't deny her attraction to Miles. In fact, she'd grown more and more enamored with him since they'd been here. But none of that mattered when their futures were meant to be separate. "Of course I like Miles. And Dylan has grown very fond of him. But we could never make a relationship work. I'm running for my life and his is here in Texas. No matter what happens, when this is over, I'll be sent to live in another city, another state. I'll take on a new name, and no one who knew me before will be allowed to know where I am. He'll stay here doing his job and protecting people."

"He could come with you."

She'd already considered that scenario, but she couldn't ask that of him. "You don't realize what you're saying, Kellyanne. For him to come with me, he would have to enter the witness protection program. He'd have to leave his job and his family behind and he would never be able to see or speak with any of you ever again."

Kellyanne's hopeful expression soured. Melissa couldn't blame her. It wasn't a life anyone would want for someone they loved. She had no family left to mourn or miss her, but Miles would be missed terribly by his family. She could never ask him to make that big of a sacrifice. And even if they somehow worked all this out, found the WITSEC mole and captured Kirby and Shearer, she could never trust a man with so many secrets. "Besides, I've been lied to my whole life. I could never really trust a man who is so comfortable being deceptive, even toward those he loves."

The door opened and Dylan rushed inside, called her name and leaped into her arms. "Mama, Grandpa John let me feed one of the horses. He took a sugar cube from my hand."

"He did? That's wonderful." Her mind went back to the terrible incident in the horse pen. She was surprised Dylan would go anywhere near the horses after that. She wasn't sure she ever would, but she realized that was probably the very reason John had taken Dylan, so he wouldn't be scared and traumatized for the rest of his life.

A tear slipped from her cheek as she realized what a nice thing that was to do. These people were always thinking of her child and had fully accepted them both, despite the lies. They were good and decent people, and she was sad that she wasn't a part of this amazing family.

She hugged Dylan to her. She didn't want to leave this place. She might not be completely safe here, but she was loved and loved everyone. She couldn't have wished for a better home for her and Dylan if she'd dreamed it—couldn't have dreamed it if she'd tried, because she'd had nothing to compare it to except for holiday movies and TV shows that she'd been sure were cheesy and unrealistic. But here, at the Silver Star Ranch, this family was something right from a movie. They'd gathered around one of their own in order to protect her. It didn't matter that she wasn't really a part of this family. They still made her feel loved and accepted. For weeks, she'd been wondering where God was when her life was being turned upside down. She was beginning to see His hand in all of this. But she still didn't understand His plan, or how He could turn this to good. Once Miles uncovered who the leak in the marshals service was, she and Dylan would be shipped off to another town to start a new life. She couldn't move to wipe away a tear.

"Mama, what wrong?" Dylan asked.

She held him closer and assured him everything was fine. But inside, she was dying at the thought of leaving the Silver Star. Of leaving the Avery family.

Of leaving Miles.

Why bring me here and show me everything I've ever wanted if it can never be mine?

Her heart cried out to God at the unfairness and a bitterness took hold of her heart.

Kellyanne joined her on the bed and pulled them both into a hug.

"Griffin, I need you to tell me you've found the leak."

His boss's sigh of frustration was not what he wanted to hear. "Not yet. I've been conducting background checks and going through each marshal's client log, but so far, I haven't found any anomalies that would lead me to think one of them is a mole."

Miles pinched the bridge of his nose as frustration burst through him. "There has to be another way to find out who is behind this."

"Is something wrong?"

"Yes, someone shot at and nearly killed us. They know where we are and I have no idea how they found us."

"Then you have no choice but to pack up and leave. Keeping this witness alive is your number-one priority."

He understood that, but the fact that his boss couldn't nail down the leak in the WITSEC program didn't instill him with confidence that Melissa would be any safer elsewhere. And Melissa was right when she'd told him if they left and were found again, they would be on their own. At least here at the Silver Star, he had his family to help keep her and Dylan safe.

He hung up with Griffin, frustrated that the man wasn't making any progress. He stepped into the house and was confronted with his family. From the looks on his parents' faces, they'd been informed about his situation.

Miles rubbed his face and took in a long, deep breath. He'd dreaded the day his family found out his secret, but a part of him was glad the truth was finally out there.

He lowered himself into a chair as he stared at the stunned expressions on their faces. Obviously, they'd never expected him to be so deceitful and secretive. His sister was the first to respond.

"I can't believe you could keep something like this from us, Miles. I thought we were closer than that."

"We *are* close, but my job—"

"No, don't use your job to try to justify this. We're family."

"And knowing the truth puts you in danger. Loving you means wanting to shield you from that."

Paul stood. "We can take care of ourselves, in case you haven't noticed. And we can help keep Melissa and Dylan safe."

He rubbed his face again. "You don't understand. Someone is after Melissa and, sure, you can help. But knowing my secret, knowing about my job? It's better for me to seal it off from my personal life as much as possible. I don't tell the people under my protection my real name, and I don't tell the people I love my real job. There are good reasons for that—first and foremost, the people I deal with are dangerous. They're not all innocent victims like Melissa and Dylan. Most of them are criminals who would do whatever it took to protect themselves. If they knew about you, it would compromise me and my ability to do my job. The best way to make sure they don't find out is to make sure as few people as possible know the full story of who I am and what I do."

"Well, we can't unknow it," his father commented. "What should we do?"

"Never tell anyone. I mean it. No one outside this house can ever know."

His mother turned away. "I don't like secrets." She was a strong woman, but worrying about her children was just a part of who she was, and now, this revelation gave her one more thing to worry about.

"I know you don't, but I love my job. I can't imagine doing anything else."

His father stood and addressed them all. "We owe it to Miles to keep this within the family. His life and his career are his business. But now we need to get back to the matter at hand. Melissa and Dylan. How can we help keep them safe?"

Miles stood and paced. His mind worked better when he was on his feet. "I don't want to leave here. I still believe the Silver Star is the best place to keep them safe. But we've obviously been compromised. Somehow, someone has come onto our property and tried to kill them. We have to lock down the ranch. No one in or out that we don't know and trust."

They all agreed. He couldn't do any better than his family, but he still wished Lawson and Colby were there as additional backup. What they were about to do— attempt to capture a paid assassin—was dangerous. Even though Josh was the sheriff and Paul had infiltrated enemy camps and rescued people during his time with the Navy SEALs, his father was still recovering from a heart attack six months ago and his mother and sister would be no match for Richard Kirby. Besides, they still had that unidentified WITSEC informant and a mob boss to deal with, too.

A truck pulled into the yard and Miles reached for his weapon, startling his mother. He started to apologize, but didn't. They would figure out that locking down the Silver Star meant not taking any chances.

He spotted Josh hopping from the driver's side of his truck as the passenger door opened and another man exited. Together they headed for the house.

"Who is this with Josh?" Miles asked.

His dad hurried to the window. "That's Zeke. He's worked for us off and on for the past several years part-time while he attends school. You know Zeke."

He remembered him, but he hadn't recognized him right away. The kid had filled out since Miles had seen him this past summer.

Josh and Zeke entered the house and both removed their cowboy hats. "I need to talk to you," Josh told Miles. "It's important."

"You can tell us all," his dad chimed in. "After all, we don't have secrets in this family. Not anymore."

Miles rolled his eyes at his father's jab. Fine, it was going to take time for his family to forgive him. He got that. "What's up?" he asked Josh.

"You remember Zeke?"

"Sure." He reached and shook the young man's hand. "How are you doing, Zeke?"

"I'm good." He fidgeted with his hat in his hands and shifted nervously from foot to foot.

"Zeke came to me with some information," Josh explained, then nudged the boy. "Go on. You tell them."

"I don't want you to think I'm the type of person who hangs out with criminals or anything because I don't. I just know a lot of people around town and, well... they approached me. I thought you should know and I called Josh just as soon as I could without drawing any suspicion."

"What's going on, Zeke? What are you talking about? Who approached you?"

"It was just some guys I know from one of my classes. They know I work at the ranch part-time and I guess they thought I would see it as an easy way to make some fast cash."

Miles didn't like the way this conversation was going. Zeke was being evasive, although it didn't appear it was on purpose. "Why don't you tell us what these guys wanted from you."

"Well, they wanted me to kidnap your wife."

His heart sank at the young man's words. "Kidnap Melissa? Why? For what reason?"

"I don't know. There's a man in town who's been approaching local gang members. They've put a price on her head. They're willing to pay anyone who can get to her."

"And these friends of yours thought you'd hand her over?"

"Well, I guess they knew I could get close without anyone getting suspicious. After all, it wouldn't be strange to see me around here, and why would some-one like me want to kidnap Melissa Avery?"

Miles didn't like this one bit. He'd asked the same question of the boys in the bunkhouse, and now he knew the answer. Money was the only reason anyone needed. And if someone was in town offering up money for Melissa, it meant the danger could be coming from anywhere and anyone. Zeke might have been honorable enough to come to Josh with the information, but that didn't mean others would balk at kidnapping, if the re-ward was great enough.

He looked at Josh, who only sighed. "That explains why all the attacks against her haven't been direct threats." Until last night. Until Kirby had decided to take matters into his own hands. "They were kids try-ing to make some quick cash."

"By threatening my family."

"Don't you mean your witness?" Kellyanne asked, correcting him.

He turned to glare at her, a reminder not to speak of Melissa as his witness in front of others. Even though he'd known Zeke practically since the kid was born, that didn't mean he was trustworthy. After all, he ap-parently hung out with friends who saw absolutely noth-ing wrong with setting fires or leaving a little kid to be trampled by a bunch of spooked horses in order to get to her in the chaos. At least, he assumed that was the reason. Even if the boy was well-intentioned, he might accidentally let something slip.

He was glad Melissa was upstairs with Dylan and not a part of this conversation.

Miles watched the kid. He continued to look nervous, and even after setting down the cowboy hat, he rubbed his hands nervously on his jeans.

His dad made a pot of coffee and offered Zeke a cup, which he took, and they all sat down.

"So tell me how you know these guys who made you the offer."

Zeke shrugged. "Like I said, we hang out sometimes. They're not bad guys, just looking to have fun."

"And kidnapping a woman is having fun?"

Zeke paled. "No. I didn't mean it that way. I just meant, they sometimes do drugs to have fun so they know some rough types. They hear things. I don't think they would have really gone through with it."

Miles had way too much experience with people who hadn't meant for a crime to go too far. Often they were the very ones he helped protect when they got in over their heads and had to make plea deals to turn on the bigger fishes. They hadn't meant to become criminals, but the temptation of easy money was often just too strong to resist. Yet, this kid had chosen to do the right thing. Miles admired that.

"Can you identify the man who made this offer?"

"No, I've never met him. When my friends approached me, I said I wasn't interested."

But Josh had other ideas. It appeared he wanted Zeke to work for them. "Can you find out from these friends of yours how much they're offering and who is making the offer?"

Zeke shrugged. "I can try. I suppose I can go back to them and say I've changed my mind. They know I need the money. I've been bumming rides from them ever since my transmission conked out on me two weeks ago."

But Miles was hesitant to ask this of Zeke. Josh had the best of intentions, but he had no idea the kind of people who were after Melissa. Shearer and his men were hard-core dangerous and Kirby was a killer. He could never ask a twenty-two-year-old college kid to take on that sort of risk.

"I think he can handle it," Josh responded when Miles questioned the plan.

"I don't mind," Zeke said. "I hate to see anyone get hurt, especially after how good the Avery family has been to me."

"And no one wants to see you get hurt, either," Miles assured him.

Josh stood. "This is a serious development, Miles. We need to get in front of it and if Zeke is willing—"

"He's a kid. We can't involve him in this."

Zeke stood and faced Miles. "I understand you don't know me that well, Miles, but you should know that I'll do almost anything I can to help this family. To help you." He slipped on his cowboy hat and headed for the door. "I'll find out who is behind this and, don't worry, Miles, I won't let anything happen to your wife."

He walked out before Miles could protest again. Not that he thought it would do any good. Zeke seemed determined.

Josh slipped his hat back on his head and also headed out. "I'll keep in constant contact with Zeke."

Miles followed Josh out the door and onto the porch.

He had a feeling that, if Zeke lived, he was about to have another witness who needed protection.

Miles paced the conference room at the sheriff's office while Josh and Cecile readied a recorder on the table. Paul leaned against a wall in the corner and Melissa sat waiting at the table. He didn't like having her here and didn't think she needed to hear this, but she'd insisted on being present.

"These are the recordings Zeke took when he approached his friends," Cecile told them. "They, in turn, took him to the guy who had made the offers."

"Were you able to capture him?" Miles asked, hoping for a quick resolution to his problem.

"No," Josh said. "But we recorded his conversation with Zeke and he's definitely placed a target on Melissa's head. He's still offering a reward for anyone who can kill her or bring her to him. I've got Zeke working with a sketch artist, but it was dark and he said the guy kept to the shadows."

As Cecile hit the button to start playing the recording, Melissa leaned forward, obviously having a difficult time making out what was being said.

Miles heard Zeke's voice asking questions and another man responding. Something about his voice seemed familiar, but Miles couldn't quite place it.

"Are you certain you can get close enough to her to grab her?" the man asked Zeke.

"I've worked for the family for years so they know me. They won't suspect anything if I'm around."

"Good. You do that. Grab her. Kill her if you can. If you can't, bring her to me and I'll take care of it."

Miles didn't like the coldness in the speaker's voice. This was all business for him and, whoever he was, he wouldn't hesitate to kill Melissa if given another chance. He might have been the one shooting at them on the road after his accomplices ran them into a tree.

"There's a time limit for this job. It needs to be handled quickly. The first person who brings her to me gets the prize."

Whoever this man was, he knew things about Melissa and about the Silver Star. But how had he known Melissa would be at the ranch? Miles still didn't understand that. Even with a mole in WITSEC, the information that he was on the case, and where his family could be found, should not have been available to them. How then were they receiving their information?

"How did you know she was here in town?" Zeke asked the very question Miles had been wondering himself and the man growled at him.

"That's not your concern. Do your job and collect your money. It's as simple as that."

The recording ended and Cecile clicked it off. Melissa sighed and sat back in her seat. Miles could see how listening to someone offering money for her life had her shaken. "Are you okay?" he asked.

She nodded, but then pushed back her chair and stood. "I think I'll go check on Dylan." They'd placed Dylan in Josh's office when they'd arrived and asked the receptionist to keep an eye on him.

He nodded. "I think that's a good idea." She left the

room and Miles turned back to his brothers and Cecile. "Zeke did good. Did you show him the photo of Kirby?"

"I did," Josh stated. "He said it wasn't the guy he met with. I also showed him Shearer's photo, too, just in case, but it wasn't him, either. In fact, he couldn't identify him as any of Shearer's known associates. He described the guy as in his thirties, tall and athletic with dark hair but, again, it was dark and this guy made certain Zeke didn't get a good look at his face. I doubt he'll be able to give us a good enough sketch."

"Shearer isn't the type to do his own dirty work, but I can't believe it wasn't Kirby." Griffin had said Kirby had gone underground, but he certainly had the most to lose since Melissa could identify him as the man who'd murdered her mother. But Shearer had other men on his payroll, including whoever was leaking him WITSEC information. Was he the one leading the attacks against Melissa? If so, they had to uncover his identity soon.

"Whoever this guy is, he's careful," Cecile told them. "He blasted a vague but pointed notice on social media, but made sure it didn't lead back to anyone in particular. We traced the user name he used to a fake account and the IP address to a local library in Dallas, where he signed in under a fake name. He's using a cloned phone for text messages. He's covering his tracks."

"Maybe, but he'll have to show up in person to collect Melissa," Paul stated.

"What are you saying?" Josh asked him.

"Have Zeke message him that he's kidnapped Melissa and is ready to hand her off. He'll have to show up then."

"Or he might send someone else to pick her up," Josh argued.

"Either way," Cecile commented, "it would be putting her in danger's way."

Miles gaped at his brother, appalled that they were even discussing the possibility. No way was he placing Melissa into the hands of a known killer even if it meant bringing the guy in. Too many things could go wrong. He wouldn't risk it.

"Not if it's not her," Paul continued. He turned to Cecile. "You and Melissa are about the same height and build. With a wig, it could fool him, at least until you got close enough to arrest him."

She considered it, then nodded. "That's a decent plan. And if we make me up to look like I've been beaten up, that would help hide my face even more."

Josh stood stoically. "That's asking a lot of Zeke."

But Cecile stood to face him. "He's the one who wanted to do this. I would be right there with him. Plus, you and your brothers would be close by. I'm not saying it isn't dangerous, but it's the job we signed on for, isn't it?"

Josh nodded. "Okay. Bring Zeke in. I want him under my protection until this goes down."

Cecile hurried out of the conference room.

Miles studied his brother. He saw hesitation in his face—hesitation to put people he cared about in the line of fire. He understood that. "Are you sure you want to do this? It's not too late to back out."

"Cecile is right. This is the job."

Miles didn't like this idea much, but if they were

truly going to capture this guy, he agreed it was time to act. And using Cecile to lure this guy out of the darkness was the best plan he'd heard so far. Best of all, it might mean they could resolve this soon and end the danger to Melissa. No matter what else happened, he wasn't going to allow anyone to hurt her. Like his brother, he wasn't ready to lose anyone he cared about.

He walked out of the conference room and into Josh's office. Melissa looked up at him. He probably shouldn't have brought her—or Dylan—with him to the sheriff's office, but he'd decided he wasn't ready to let either of them out of his sight. He preferred having them where he could protect them both and he couldn't do that if he was across town.

"What did you all decide?" she asked.

"They're going to have Cecile pretend to be you and have Zeke deliver her to this guy who offered to pay him. By the way, it wasn't Kirby."

"Who do you think it is?"

"I don't know. The mole in my office, maybe. Whoever they are, this could tie him back to Kirby and Shearer—and then you would be safe."

"Do you think that will work?"

"I don't know. Maybe. I hope it does."

"That Zeke is a pretty brave kid, isn't he?"

"Yeah, I'm just now realizing what a good guy he really is. Are you going to be okay in here or would you rather we return to the Silver Star?" He preferred staying here, but it looked like it was going to be a long night monitoring the situation with Zeke and Cecile, and it might be easier to care for Dylan at the ranch.

But, hopefully, once it was over, this nightmare would be over, too, and Melissa would be free from danger.

She rubbed Dylan's hair as she looked up at Miles. "I'd rather stay close."

He was glad. The sheriff's office would be on minimal staff with five of the eight deputies involved in the operation, but Melissa was still safer here with him and his brothers close by than she would be anywhere else. "We'll be in the conference room if you need us and I've got my cell phone. I'll be checking on you."

He headed back toward the conference room, where Cecile was pulling on the wig that would transform her into a reasonably convincing copy of Melissa. He had to admit, from a distance, she could pass. It was a good plan and he was hopeful. He grabbed a cup of coffee and was surprised to find Ellie sitting at one of the tables in the break room. He hadn't seen his old girlfriend since he and Melissa had bought those clothes from her when they'd first come to town. "Hey, Ellie, what's going on? Why are you here?"

"Someone tried to…break into my house this afternoon." Her words came out choppy and he noticed how anxious she seemed as she gripped a paper cup full of coffee. "I came home from the grocery store and found him. Deputy Vance asked me to come in and file a report and look through some mug shots to see if I can identify the guy, but it seems everyone is busy with something else."

Normal operations had been affected by this sting operation and he felt bad she was being inconvenienced by it. "I'm sure someone will be able to help you soon."

"It doesn't matter. I really don't want to be alone in that house right now. I'm just as happy to stay here for a while."

He kneeled beside her and felt her shaking. She'd had a frightening experience and was fortunate the intruder hadn't harmed her. He felt like a jerk now for bringing up her marriage back when they'd run into each other in the store. It wasn't until he'd spoken with his mother later that he'd learned that not only was she divorced, but she'd also lost her four-year-old son in a drowning accident. As bad as things had gotten for her, he was surprised she'd returned to Courtland County, but perhaps this community could be what helped her cope with her losses.

He understood that, too. His hometown was important to him, as well. He glanced through the office windows to where Melissa was reading Dylan a book on Josh's couch and felt a familiar pull. This place was home, but so was she.

Ellie followed his gaze. "Is that Melissa in Josh's office?"

"Yeah, she and Dylan are hanging out while we take care of some business with my brother."

"Maybe I'll stop in and keep her company until Vance is ready for me."

"I think she would like that." And he liked that Melissa wouldn't be alone.

Ellie reached for his hand. "You're a good man, Miles Avery. I'm happy I got to see you again."

He wished her well then headed back into the conference room, but not before spotting another sight in the hallway that caught him off guard—Zeke leaning down to plant a kiss on Miles's sister. Kellyanne spotted him watching as Zeke hurried for the conference room. Her face flushed when she realized Miles had seen them.

She locked eyes with him and shrugged as if it was no big deal. "You're not the only one with secrets, you know."

But yet, she'd been the one to read him the riot act when his secrets had come to light.

"Zeke has been asking me out since we were in high school together, but I was never interested before."

"What changed your mind?" Miles asked her.

"I see a lot of bad things, a lot of bad people, in my job. I suppose I finally realized I shouldn't turn away a good man when I see one." She glanced into the conference room, where Zeke was being fitted with a recording device, and Miles realized she was worried about him. He saw affection shining in her expression and was happy for her. She was right. Zeke was one of the good guys. "Don't worry," he said, trying to reassure her. "Josh and Cecile won't let anything happen to him."

"I know. But I'm going to stick around just in case." She hurried down the hall toward Josh's office and he saw her kneel down to play with Dylan on the floor. He was glad Melissa had decided to stay. They all needed a distraction tonight.

Melissa chatted with Kellyanne and briefly with Ellie before Deputy Vance called her out to look at mug shots. The whole time, Melissa's attention was never far away from what was happening miles away and being observed in the conference room. She wished she was in there watching, too, but she didn't think she could stand seeing an image of herself being handed over to a killer. It wasn't real, but that didn't stop fear from pressing down on her. She knew that if she watched it, she wouldn't be able to stop the constant replay in her head of the moment she'd found her mother's lifeless body and then realized the killer was still inside the house, and every other life-threatening incident since then. She was weary of it all and she preferred to just stay here in this office with Dylan, where they were safe from the madness that was happening in the world.

She turned back to see Kellyanne playing dinosaurs with Dylan, who was giggling and having a good time. He wasn't bothered with being cooped up in this office because he had people around him who played with him and cared about him. Kellyanne would have made a good aunt to Dylan and she wished that he would have a family like the Averys. But that could never happen. She had to enjoy it while it lasted, before she and Dylan moved on to their next identity and said goodbye to both Miles and the Avery family for good.

She grew a little light-headed at the thought of saying goodbye and sat on the couch before her legs gave out. She always did her best to keep her emotions in check, especially in front of Dylan, so this reaction was disconcerting. But she soon realized this was more than just her emotions gone wild. The room started spinning and she felt sick. She tried to call out to Kellyanne, but saw her lying unmoving on the carpet as Dylan played beside her.

Something was wrong. Kellyanne wouldn't have fallen asleep like that. She glanced at the coffee cups sitting around the room and realized someone must have drugged them. She tried to reach for one and knocked it over, spilling the contents on the floor, but she couldn't muster the strength to clean up the mess. Her limbs had grown heavy and she was having trouble keeping her eyes open.

She tried to call out to Dylan and after a moment he walked over to her and looked at her questioningly.

"Mama, you okay?"

She wanted to reassure him, but at the same time she knew something was terribly wrong. She tried to scream at him to run and hide, but the words wouldn't come. The door opened and Dylan turned to someone who picked him up. She couldn't see who it was, but she was screaming in her head.

Help me! Please, help me!

She tried to turn her head to see what was happening and caught only a glimpse of Dylan's face as someone carried him out the door before the darkness pulled her away.

NINE

Miles paced while his brothers watched surveillance video from a camera pinned to a button on Cecile's blouse. He was surprised Josh's small department could afford video surveillance, but his brother had told him the cameras had been purchased with money confiscated during a drug bust. He listened to Cecile walk Zeke through what they were about to do before Zeke pulled the car to a stop and they both stepped into character.

Zeke dragged a struggling Cecile toward a parked dark-colored SUV. The kid was a good actor and really seemed to be playing his part to the letter. Cecile kept her head down until they approached the car, but the camera on her shirt had a clear line of vision as a man exited the vehicle and approached them.

"I have what you wanted," Zeke told him.

Two more men got out of the SUV—one from the back seat and another the front passenger side. This last man walked around the front of the car and approached them. The camera picked up his image, but thanks to the hat he was wearing, there was no clear shot of his face. He was also the first one to realize the ruse.

"It's not her! It's a trap," he hollered as Cecile pulled out her weapon and warned them all to freeze.

"Go now," Josh commanded the backup team.

The man in the hat took off running just as the team arrived.

Cecile darted after him, shouting for him to stop, but the man quickly outdistanced her and disappeared in a matter of minutes.

"We need a team to block off the streets and get a team out here to find this guy," Cecile said into her microphone.

Josh responded. "Already on the way. Did you get a good look at him? Was he the man in charge?"

"I think so," she said between heavy breaths. "The guys we captured appeared to be just muscle. And, no, I didn't get a good look at him. He had his cap low, so it was difficult to see his features."

Josh pushed back from the table. "I'm heading out there. You guys coming with me?"

Paul nodded and stood. "Absolutely. I can't arrest anyone, but I'll do what I can to help with the search."

But Miles shook his head. Their best opportunity to catch this guy had turned sour and he had to think about Melissa and Dylan. Protecting them was his number-one job. "I'm going to take Melissa and Dylan home. You'll let me know if you find anything?"

Josh agreed. Miles doubted they would find the guy, but even if they did, it would take more than arresting him to end this. They also had to convince him to turn against Shearer and admit that Shearer was the one who had pulled all the strings to have Melissa eliminated. Otherwise, Melissa might never be free from danger.

He headed for Josh's office and noticed as he approached that the blinds were closed. He opened the door and walked inside to see Melissa slumped over on the couch in an unnatural manner. His sister was in a similar state on the floor. Paper cups and what looked like coffee had been spilled. Dylan was nowhere to be seen.

He rushed to Melissa, called her name and shook her until she groggily responded to him. There was no doubt in his mind that she'd been drugged. For a terrible moment, he wondered if he'd lost her. Panic gripped him and he shook her again until her eyes fluttered and she weakly tried to push him away. That sent relief flooding through him that, at least, she was alive.

He yelled out that he needed help as he rushed to check on Kellyanne. Several deputies came running, followed soon by Josh and Paul.

"What happened?" Josh asked, hurrying over to Kellyanne and checking on her.

"I'll call for an ambulance," Deputy Vance said, then turned and ran from the room.

Paul bent and examined the spilled coffee cups. "Looks like they've both been drugged."

Those words sent shivers through Miles and he feared the worst. "Where's Dylan?" He prayed the boy had just wandered off on his own.

The others began searching the room, then the rest

of the sheriff's office, but after an extensive search, Josh told him that they couldn't find Dylan anywhere.

"I'm having my tech team pull video surveillance to see who walked in and out of here. We'll find him. And the ambulance is on the way for these two."

He sat by Melissa's side, knowing that when she finally regained consciousness, she was going to be devastated. How could he have let this happen?

And how was he ever going to break the news to her that Dylan was missing?

Melissa's head was still swimming even as she awoke. She fought her way back to consciousness and forced her eyelids to open. She'd heard a lot of commotion and realized she was lying on the couch in Josh's office.

She recognized Miles's deep voice close by, but she couldn't see him. Memories began to return and she recalled feeling light-headed, then realizing that she'd been drugged before passing out. Then Dylan's face as he was carried away from her. She cried out.

Miles was by her side in a flash, kneeling on the floor. "Melissa, are you okay?"

Hot, pressing sobs racked her. "Where's my baby?" she moaned, but he had no answer. Dylan was gone. She knew it in her heart.

He gripped her shoulders and forced her to sit up, which helped clear her head. "I need you to focus." His tone was sharp and demanding. "What happened here? Did you see who took Dylan?"

She saw horror and fear manifesting in his eyes and

forced herself to push aside her emotions and try to focus, but all she could see, all she could remember, was Dylan's face as he was carried away. "I—I don't know. I didn't see the person."

His fingers dug into her shoulders. "Was it a man or woman? Tall or short? Did you notice anything about them? A sound? A smell? Anything?"

"I don't know," she cried, pushing his hands away. He acted like he was the one whose child was missing. Then she remembered she hadn't been alone. "Kelly-anne. She was here with me. Is she all right?"

"She's fine. She's being questioned by Josh. Unfortunately, she doesn't remember anything, either. It looks like someone drugged you both."

Someone had planned this—drugging their coffees, then watching and waiting for them both to pass out before snatching her child from her.

"It doesn't make sense. Why take Dylan and not you?"

She tried to stand, but her legs were still shaky. Miles lowered her back to the couch. "The paramedics want to take you both to the emergency room to get you checked out," he said.

"I'm not going," she declared. "I want to know what's happening, what's being done to find Dylan." She couldn't sit around doing nothing. She needed to be out there looking for her child.

She tried to push to her feet, but once again, her legs buckled beneath her.

Miles's arms went around her, keeping her from falling. She turned and leaned into him as hot, angry tears burst through her and sobs racked her body.

Where was her baby?

Melissa sat on the couch in Josh's office with a blanket over her shoulders as the paramedic took her blood pressure. She looked pale and ready to faint. He hated seeing her this way and longed to go to her and comfort her, but he had another job to do. He had to find Dylan.

Melissa was refusing to go to the hospital, as was Kellyanne. They were both determined to stay at the sheriff's office to help, but there wasn't really anything they could do, since neither could recall seeing the person who had taken Dylan.

He met up with Josh in the surveillance room for an update, but his brother didn't have much to offer. "We've been through all the video footage and we can't find any images of anyone leaving the building with Dylan. We expanded our search to the courthouse and the surrounding areas, too, but not all the video-surveillance equipment is working. We had a tornado that swept through here a few months ago and it did a lot of damage to video cameras that haven't yet all been replaced. But we're reaching out to the local shops in the square, as well as spreading the word in case someone in one of them saw something."

Miles rubbed a hand through his hair. How could someone just pick up a three-year-old boy and take off with him without someone noticing? For that matter, how could someone drug Melissa and his sister in order to make that happen? He glanced around the sheriff's office. They'd been on minimal staff last night because of the sting operation, but this still should have been a safe place. Someone had to have been watching them, waiting for the opportunity to strike. But why take Dylan when Melissa was clearly Shearer's target?

"We've set up roadblocks in and out of town and I've got the sheriffs and local law-enforcement offices in the surrounding counties on alert, too."

Josh was doing all he could and Paul was already out searching for Dylan, but it wasn't enough. This department was already stretched thin with the sting operation and processing the men they'd arrested. As Cecile had suspected, the men were low-level muscle, probably Shearer's men but, so far, they weren't talking.

Miles should have had his agency, his marshal friends and his partner, Lanie, to call upon. The US Marshals Service had more resources to draw on than Josh and his county sheriff's office, but he couldn't call them for fear of bringing the danger to them. But then Shearer had found Melissa and Dylan already. Did it really matter now who the leak was when whoever it was had already sold them out and brought danger right to his family?

"I need to call my boss," Miles stated. He pulled out his phone and dialed Griffin's number. "Something has happened." He explained everything, including that they were staying at his family's ranch. He endured the lecture from Griffin for diverging from procedure, giving his reasons for staying close to his family after the shooting and promising that he would accept any consequences for his actions. But then he dug into his real reason for calling—the fact that Shearer, Kirby or their associates had found a horrific new way to strike against Melissa. "Dylan has been taken. Melissa and my sister were drugged by whoever took him."

He heard his boss's frustrated sigh on the other end. "We haven't had any leads on the leak and so far we have no reason to believe anyone from the marshals service knew your whereabouts. If someone was able to connect you to the case, or track Melissa to your location, then they've managed to do it without raising any red flags. I can send you backup, but I'd be doing it blindly, since there's no way of knowing who in the office can be trusted. If you feel like you need our intervention then you'll have it, but remember your number-one priority is to the witness, keeping her safe from the men who are after her. Anyone I send might be the source of increased danger for her. I'm working on leaking some information to try to weed out the leak in the office. I'll let you know if anything comes of it."

"Thanks, Griffin." He hung up and walked over to Melissa. He sat with her and put his arm around her, and she leaned into him as tears flowed down her face. None of this made sense. If this was Shearer and he had Dylan, his only play now was to use Dylan to lure Melissa to him or threaten to kill him if she testified. But why take Dylan when he could have just killed Melissa right then and there? He couldn't hold the boy indefinitely. None of this made sense. His plan had to be to lure her to him and, if that was the case, they would soon be getting a message from him.

"I need to ask you a question," he said. "Shearer

might have taken Dylan to use him as bait to capture you. I need you to tell me if he calls you, Melissa. If he somehow manages to get a message to you, promise me that you'll tell me. Promise that you won't sneak off and try to rescue him alone." He gripped her arms and she struggled against him. He should be gentler, but his fear was that she would leave him out of the loop.

He'd seen how instinctively she acted to protect her son—whether there were bullets flying at them or horse hooves coming down near their heads. She didn't stop to think and she didn't hesitate. She'd see her son in danger and she'd jump to shield him in any way she could. If a threatening message came to her—"Meet me at this address or your son dies," perhaps—then he worried she'd act automatically, without stopping to think of the consequences. Then they both would be gone and he knew what that meant. They would both be dead. "Promise me."

She cried out and jerked her arms from his grip. "Stop it, you're hurting me."

He released her and took a deep breath. "I'm sorry. That wasn't my intention. I just need your word that you won't leave without me. You won't try to sneak away."

He saw her eyes darting back and forth. She was thinking, trying to figure out something. Finally, she looked at him, tears pooling in her eyes. "I'm sorry, Miles. I can't make that promise. I'll do whatever I have to do to get him back."

"No, you don't understand. Giving in to that kind of blackmail won't save anyone. Once Shearer has you, you'll both be killed."

"I can't risk it. I have to do whatever they say. They have my baby. My baby! You have no idea what it's like to have your child jerked from your arms. I want him back! I want him back safely!"

"I know you do. We will get him back. I promise."

Her eyes darted to his. "Don't you promise that, Miles. You don't get to make me any promises." Her next words cut him to his core. "You promised to keep us safe and you failed! You failed, Miles. My baby is gone because of you! Because you couldn't do your job." She stormed into the office and slammed the door shut hard enough to rattle the pictures on the walls.

He hung his head and took a long, deep breath to try to contain the anguish building up inside him. She was right about him. He'd failed to do his job. He'd failed to keep them both safe. Even though he knew she was just lashing out, she was still right. He was a failure. He put his head in his hands. His heart was breaking, ripping in two. He couldn't keep her safe, couldn't keep her from sneaking away, and still search for Dylan. He could let Josh and the others take the lead on finding the boy, but he didn't want to. He loved that kid, had grown to love him so much that he wanted to be there, involved in the search for him. But what could he do? He couldn't leave her alone, either, and risk losing them both.

He stood and walked down the hallway, stopping at the door to Josh's office. He saw her silhouette leaning against it and even from that angle he could see her shoulders shaking as she cried. He didn't knock but leaned against the door and spoke through it. His voice cracked with emotion that he couldn't hold back.

"I'm sorry I let you down. I never meant to. I made you a promise to keep you and Dylan safe and you're right, I failed. But I *will* find him, Melissa. I will bring him back to you. That's a promise I will keep." He turned and walked back to the command center.

Right now, finding Dylan was his main concern. He could only pray that Melissa would give him one more chance to prove himself, that she wouldn't try to take matters into her own hands.

Melissa couldn't breathe. Anger and fear pressed against her chest and her arms ached to hold her baby. She couldn't imagine the horror he was enduring and each moment that passed without news was devastating.

That was why she couldn't make that promise to Miles. She would go to Kirby or Shearer or whoever in an instant if it meant Dylan could live. She begged God for that phone call, but hours passed and it didn't come.

She knew they were doing all they could to find Dylan, but knowing that someone got close enough to spike their drinks meant they could get to her no matter where she went. No one could keep her safe from these men, not even Miles, no matter how much he tried.

A figure appeared in the doorway and she turned and saw Kellyanne standing there. She fell onto the couch beside Melissa and threw her arms around her as her own set of tears erupted. "I'm sorry. I don't know what happened. One minute I was fine, and the next, someone was shaking me awake and Dylan was gone."

Melissa assured her she didn't blame her. Someone had drugged them both, but it hadn't been Kellyanne's responsibility to protect Dylan. It had been hers. Hers and Miles's. She pulled out her mother's necklace and pressed it against her lips. She needed to feel close to her when everything was falling apart.

Kellyanne sniffed and motioned at the necklace. "What's that?"

She opened her hand and let Kellyanne see the charm and chain. "It belonged to my mother. She gave it to me on my twenty-fifth birthday and I've worn it ever since. Now that she's gone, holding it helps me to feel closer to her." And she needed that comfort now with Dylan gone more than ever. She wished her mother was here to tell her what to do.

Kellyanne looked confused. "The only thing I know about the witness protection program is you're not supposed to keep anything that can be linked to your past, right?"

Melissa felt her face redden with embarrassment that Kellyanne had uncovered her secret. "Yes, that's true. One of the marshals saw me wearing it and tried to take it from me, but I completely fell apart so he said I could keep it as long as I kept it hidden."

"So Miles doesn't know you have this?"

She shook her head, realizing she'd been condemning him for his need for secrecy when all the while she'd been keeping this from him.

"You should tell him," Kellyanne commented. "He's been going crazy trying to figure out how these people found you. It might not be connected to this, but you still owe him the truth about this necklace."

"I'm sure it's nothing."

"But what if it isn't?"

Melissa glanced through the office's windows at Miles, who was deep in conversation with his brothers. Perhaps even now he was trying to wrap his brain around how Shearer's men had found them. The truth in Kellyanne's insistence hit home for her. Kellyanne was right. She'd kept this necklace from him.

At best, her necklace had nothing to do with any of this and she was about to tell him something unimportant. At worst, he would take the last possession she had of her mother and she would never see it again.

Still, she felt a loyalty to Miles after all he'd done to protect them. She had to tell him the complete truth.

She got up and approached Miles as he was talking to his brothers. "I need to tell you something," she said when he saw her.

His brothers moved away to give them some privacy and Miles turned back to Melissa. "What is it? Did you remember something?" He folded his arms, his presence distant and that hurt even though she knew he was only reacting to what she'd said earlier.

"No, I didn't." She sniffed back tears and debated the best way to begin, finally deciding it was better to just get the words out there. "I did break one of the WITSEC rules."

Anticipation clouded his eyes. "You called someone? Who?"

"No, nothing like that. It's nothing that would alert anyone to where we are, but I haven't been completely honest with you, Miles, and for that, I'm sorry." Now, the tears managed to push through and she put her hands over her mouth to catch her breath before continuing. "I just missed her so much. I haven't even had an opportunity to grieve for her."

"What is it, Melissa? Just tell me. What did you do?"

She reached into her pocket and pulled out the necklace. "They said I couldn't keep anything from my old life, but my mom gave this to me. It's the only thing I have left of her. I couldn't give it up. I'm sorry." She placed it into his hand and turned away. Would he allow her to keep it, like the other marshal had? He was certainly more compassionate and caring than the other marshals she'd encountered, but he was also much more concerned about their safety and he followed the rules. They were an important part of his life and his job and she'd violated them.

He was silent for a moment, then started to reprimand her. "Melissa—"

"I know, I know. I should have given it up. I just… couldn't. One of the marshals saw me wearing it and tried to confiscate it, but then he changed his mind when he saw how important it was to me. He said I could keep it as long as I didn't wear it and kept it hidden. I thought it would be fine. It's only a necklace. What harm could keeping it possibly do?"

She turned to look at him and saw him peeling at something on the back of the charm. He separated it from the necklace and held it up. It was flat and tiny, small enough to hide against the back of the charm without her even noticing it was there. "What is that?"

He gave a loud sigh. "It's a GPS device. It's how they've been tracking you all this time."

* * *

Melissa gasped and put her hands over her mouth as the horrible realization hit her. "I did this," she cried, having trouble catching her breath. "I did this. I led them right to us. I'm the reason they were able to capture Dylan."

He started to reach for her but pulled back, probably deciding after their talk earlier, she wouldn't welcome it. "No, don't do that to yourself. You didn't know."

"I should have known. I broke the rules, Miles. I did this. It's all on me."

"You didn't know there was a tracker on the necklace. You just wanted something of your mom's. I understand that. The real question is how did this tracker get on it? How long have you had this necklace? Has it ever not been in your possession?"

"My mother gave it to me for my twenty-fifth birthday. Up until we entered WITSEC, I wore it all the time. I never took it off."

"Which means someone bugged it while you were in WITSEC. The question is who and when."

She shook her head, trying to remember. "No one even seemed to notice it until we arrived at the hotel where you met up with us. Once we were there, one of the marshals who brought us noticed it and told me he had to take it. I handed it over, but I was upset. I went into the bathroom and cried. When I came out, he handed it back to me and told me to keep it hidden." That had to have been when the bug was placed. "I thought he was doing something nice, but he was just using me, wasn't he?"

He nodded and rubbed his jaw. "Do you remember the guy's name?"

"No, I don't."

"Would you recognize him if you saw him again?"

She tried to think back to recapture his image, but even that was futile. "He was nice to me and I appreciated that, but..." She sighed in frustration. "I've just seen so many marshals in the past month. They've all started to blur together."

"I understand." He led her to the couch and sank into the cushions beside her. "Tell me about the necklace. I want to know its history."

"I've already told you. My mother bought it for me for my birthday. I hardly ever removed it. I haven't worn it since the marshal gave it back to me—but I've kept it in my pocket." Horror and grief shuddered through her. "I led them right to Dylan."

"No, stop it. This is a good lead. I'll have my boss pull the protection-detail records. We'll figure out who did this and why, and once we do, we'll find Dylan and you'll both be safe."

She leaned into him and he cautiously placed an arm around her. She heard the steady beat of his heart. He was a good man and she'd been wrong to blame him but this incident only proved that her initial opinion of secrets had been right all along. Secrets were wrong and she could never be with someone who couldn't share his life fully and freely with her. That realization broke her heart. She'd fallen for him. She knew it. Despite her better judgment, his kindness had surprised her and opened her guarded heart enough to let him inside. Miles was everything she would want in a husband and everything she could ask for in a father for Dylan. But there were just too many obstacles between them.

Beginning with her missing child.

Miles took out his phone and dialed his boss's number. Finally, he had a lead—even if it was one that infuriated him. He hated that Melissa had been betrayed once again by the marshals service. They'd promised to protect her, but instead, someone had used her and tracked her location.

He updated Griffin about the necklace and the marshal who'd allowed her to keep it and, in Miles's opinion, had planted a bug on it.

"She doesn't remember the name of the marshal, but she did say it was a man." Eliminating the female marshals was a good start and, at least, that meant Lanie was no longer suspect. That was some good news.

"I'll send you a photo outline of each of the male marshals who worked her detail. Maybe she can point him out to us."

"I also need you to run background checks on those marshals," Miles replied. "Whoever this guy is, it's clear that he's the leak in our office."

"I've been doing my best to root him out, but so far I haven't come up with anything. Let me know if Melissa points him out."

He hung up with Griffin, but heard his phone beep a moment later. He opened an attachment from his boss and glanced through the photo display of marshals he'd known and worked with for years. His gut clenched at the idea that one of them might be a turncoat, a patsy for a mob boss. One of these men, who'd sworn to protect Melissa and Dylan, had instead sold them out.

He approached her while she was stretched out on the couch, a blanket covering her. "I'd like you to look at these photographs to see if you can point out the marshal who gave you back the necklace."

She nodded and took the phone with shaky hands. "I'll do my best."

She scrolled through several photos before she stopped on one. "That's him."

She handed the phone back to him and he glanced at the image. His heart dropped. She'd just pointed out Adam Stringer, his best friend and Lanie's boyfriend. Adam was the one to place the GPS tracker on the necklace.

He sent the image to Griffin with a short message about Melissa's identification and then he put his phone away. He leaned against the desk in the office as the weight of the truth about his life sank in. Even his secrets had secrets, and he was growing weary of them. His friend, one of the only people in the world he'd felt comfortable sharing himself with, had proven untrustworthy and placed Melissa and Dylan's lives in danger.

God, I don't know where to turn.

How could his friend have betrayed him this way? How could someone be so desperate that they would turn on a witness under their protection? He couldn't understand it, but at least now he could call in the marshals to help search for Dylan. The program still owed it to her to find her son and bring him home safely.

Griffin sent him a text message letting him know the marshals would be arriving in Courtland County by the next morning. They were bringing the full force of the United States Marshals Service with them, minus Adam Stringer, who had mysteriously gone missing and wasn't answering his cell phone.

Miles watched Melissa through the office window as she dealt with her grief over what she'd done, keeping that secret from him. His heart broke for her. He understood Melissa's dislike for secrecy and he was beginning to dislike it more and more. Could he continue doing what he did even once this was all over? The problem was that he couldn't imagine doing anything else. His job was important and the secrecy was a necessary part of it. That would never change for him. But perhaps the agency and Griffin would implement some controls that would prevent their inspectors from being so isolated that they became prime recruits for the bad guys.

Of course, any change they made in the future wouldn't do anything to help Melissa right now. The only thing the marshals service could do for her at this point was rally the forces to try to get back her son… and then send Melissa and Dylan off to start a new life somewhere. Without him.

He couldn't deny his attraction had been growing stronger and stronger with each day he'd been with her. He wanted her and Dylan in his life, but that was something that could never be. Especially not now, after he'd let her down the way he had. His only hope was to bring Dylan home to her and make certain the next place they were sent to would be safe. Keeping her alive had to be more important than keeping her with him.

But first, they had to find Dylan.

And given that Adam had gone MIA at the same time that an unknown man had begun recruiting people to kidnap Melissa, Miles suspected the man on that video had been Adam. That was why his voice had sounded so familiar on Zeke's recording.

He was going to find Adam and make sure he paid the price for his betrayal.

Miles and Melissa headed back to the Silver Star. The chasm between them stretched far and wide and felt all the more painful as he recalled how close they'd become. All that was gone now and he wondered if they could ever get it back. Perhaps it was better that they never did. He'd moved his focus from protecting Melissa to being with her, and that had caused him to overlook important details, things that had placed her and her son's life in danger. He couldn't—wouldn't—allow that to happen again.

Once they were back at the ranch, she went upstairs and locked herself into her bedroom, while Miles settled down to reread the statements and reports from Dylan's kidnapping. They still hadn't received any contact from the killer luring Melissa to him. That troubled Miles. What other purpose would they have in taking Dylan? Dylan hadn't even been in the house when Melissa's mother was killed and, even if he had been, he was too young to testify against Kirby. And besides, why kidnap Dylan when Melissa was right there, drugged and vulnerable? The perfect target. Had the drug in the drinks been meant to kill her instead of just knocking her out? That was a possibility, but as murder weapons went, it was a sloppy one. That led him back to Zeke's encounter with the mystery man, possibly Adam, who was recruiting young adults to try to harm her.

He poured over the statements taken from everyone they'd interviewed that evening. The roadblocks were still set up and other counties alerted, and an Amber Alert had been issued for Dylan, but so far no leads had come in to point them in the right direction.

He made a list of all the people who had been at the sheriff's office around the time Dylan went missing. They included Melissa, Miles, Josh, Paul, Kellyanne, Ellie, Deputy Vance, Deputy Willbrook and Deputy Turner. There had also been two food deliveries during that time, including the laced coffee that Melissa and Kellyanne ultimately drank. He knew Josh had had trouble with a former deputy back in the summer who had been secretly working for a drug runner. It was possible they were dealing with a similar situation, but he had to admit, he'd known all three of these deputies for most of his life and couldn't imagine any one of them kidnapping a child. And from what he'd heard, if anyone knew the heartbreak of losing a child, it was Ellie. She could never put another mother through that nightmare just for some quick cash.

He moved on to the delivery drivers who'd brought the food and coffee. The coffee had come from a local café around the corner that regularly delivered to the sheriff's office. Josh and the others knew both delivery drivers well and, during questioning, neither had acted suspicious, and their backgrounds didn't have any red flags.

He rubbed his hands over his face and sighed. He had to think about this differently. What if Dylan's kidnapping had nothing to do with the threats against Melissa? What if this incident wasn't a result of Kirby or Shearer plotting against her? It was a stretch, but it was a possibility he had to look at. It would explain why they'd had no contact with the kidnappers and why they hadn't killed Melissa when they'd had the opportunity.

He glanced through the list of names again.

He realized if he was going to consider the idea that someone might have kidnapped Dylan for their own personal reasons, he had to look at Ellie as a viable suspect. She'd lost a child, as well as had multiple miscarriages, if the rumor mill was to be believed. Just because someone lost a child didn't automatically make them crazy enough to snatch someone else's child, he rationalized. But Ellie had lost more than just children. She'd lost her husband through divorce and her parents the year before. She'd gone from buying high-priced clothes and living in a large home to working at Robbie's as a salesclerk. And she'd doted on Dylan when she'd seen him.

So has Kellyanne.

So has everyone who knows Dylan.

He grunted. His sister obviously wasn't a kidnapper, but he couldn't completely rule out Ellie without speaking to her first. She'd been at the sheriff's office before Dylan had been kidnapped but hadn't been there afterwards. But then neither had the food and coffee delivery drivers. They'd had to return later to be questioned but, to his knowledge, no one had been able to reach Ellie for questioning.

And while he questioned her, he could have his brother check out more nefarious reasons Dylan might have been taken.

He dialed Josh and learned he and Cecile had already investigated that angle. "I got a list of pedophiles in the area and we're in the process of accounting for all of their whereabouts, but so far, it doesn't look like any of them were anywhere near the courthouse or the sheriff's office. There were no court sessions going on that late so few people would have reason to be at the courthouse, and I think we've questioned everyone we saw on the video surveillance that was close by."

"I want to reinterview the deputies who were there, then go talk to Ellie just so I can cross her off my list." He didn't really believe she was a suspect, but she'd been there so he had to speak to her.

"Cecile is already handling those interviews, but I don't believe any of them were involved. I'll go with you to Ellie's," Josh stated. "I'll meet you at her house."

Josh rattled off the address taken from Ellie's earlier complaint about a break-in and Miles put it into his phone. He woke his dad and asked him to keep an eye out for Melissa, and his father assured him he would.

Miles drove to the address Josh had given him and found his brother already parked in the driveway. Miles got out and approached him.

"It doesn't look like anyone is at home," Josh told him, "but look what I found sitting by the outside trash."

Miles saw it was a brand-new box for a child's car seat and knew without a doubt Ellie was involved. That meant it looked less and less like this had anything to do with Kirby or Shearer or the reason Melissa was in WITSEC in the first place.

"There also don't appear to be any signs of a break-in. All the doors and windows are secure. She must have concocted that break-in story to have a reason to be at the sheriff's office."

"But how would she have known we would be there at that time?"

Josh shrugged. "Small-town gossip? At least it didn't get back to the men Zeke was meeting with."

Miles soaked it all in and tried to think where Ellie might go. Then he recalled the conversation they'd had at the general store. "She has an aunt in Dallas. We need to find out where that is."

He hoped Ellie wasn't a sophisticated enough criminal to think about covering her tracks. Or perhaps she thought they would blame whoever was after Melissa. Which they had. Truthfully, she could be anywhere, but they would start their search for her with the only family she had left.

"On it." Josh nodded, pulled out his cell phone and called the office.

Miles phoned Paul, updated him and asked him to return to the Silver Star to keep an eye on Melissa. Paul agreed. Now that he believed Dylan's kidnapping wasn't tied to Kirby or Shearer, Miles couldn't discount the possibility that they, or someone they'd hired to do their dirty work, would take advantage of his absence to try to grab her. He wanted to be there but knew she would want him to focus on bringing Dylan home first.

Lanie, Griffin, several of the other marshals in his office and a unit from the Dallas PD met them at the address Cecile had found for Ellie's aunt. Miles readied himself to enter the apartment, praying he would find Dylan unharmed. He was already looking forward to holding him again and bringing him home to Melissa.

Lanie removed her US Marshal gear and approached the apartment first, knocking on the door with a made-up story about searching for her missing cat. The woman who answered—obviously Ellie's aunt— wished her luck but stated she hadn't seen anything. Lanie thanked her, then walked back toward the group.

She nodded at Miles. "There is a child in there. I saw him sitting on the couch with a woman who looked like our suspect."

Miles thanked her, all sympathy for Ellie evaporating now that he knew she'd drugged Melissa and Kellyanne, then snatched Dylan from them. He readied his weapon, hoping he wouldn't need it but wanting to be ready in case he did.

Dallas PD led the maneuver into the apartment and by the time Miles entered, the officers were in a standoff with Ellie.

She gasped when she spotted Miles. "You can't just come in here without knocking."

But he was done talking to her. "Move away from the child, Ellie."

From behind her, he spotted a dark head poke out and a smile light up the boy's face. "Miles!"

Ellie scooped Dylan into her arms and Miles took several steps toward her, but she quickly walked backward the same distance. "Don't come any closer," she demanded, gripping the boy so tightly that he began to whimper. "I'll hurt him if you come any closer."

He shook his head. "You don't want to hurt him. He doesn't belong to you. You have to know this is wrong."

Her aunt, who'd already been detained by the local PD, cried out. "Ellie, what did you do? You told me you adopted him from a family who couldn't care for him any longer."

Ellie's face contorted. "Wrong? You have no idea what the word *wrong* means. Wasn't it wrong that I had to lose my baby? That I had to have my husband leave me? That I lost my parents? Wasn't that wrong? Don't I deserve something good in my life? Melissa has everything I've ever wanted. The husband, the child, the big loving family. Why should she get all of that when I have nothing, Miles?"

His heart broke at her words, mostly because she had no idea what Melissa had and didn't have. Melissa's tales of woe were as bad as Ellie's. She'd lost so much, too. Her mother, her home, her husband. Even her identity. All she had left was this child that Ellie had taken from her. "You don't know what you're talking about," he warned her. "You have no idea what her life is like and now you're trying to take the only good thing she has—her child."

"I've lost everything! At least she still has you, Miles."

So once again, Melissa was in this mess because of him, because of the lies and secrets he'd forced her to share. He'd made up a life for her that was built on lies, and those lies had convinced an unstable woman that Melissa was a fair target. She would never forgive him for this and that was okay. He would be satisfied enough if he could bring Dylan back to her. "I'm not letting you leave with that child. You may as well hand him over."

She clung to him and Dylan began to cry. He squirmed and called Miles's name, reaching for him. "Miles! Miles, help me!" He managed to wriggle away from her and slide to the floor, running toward Miles before she could grab him again.

Ellie's shoulders slumped as Miles scooped Dylan into his arms and hugged him, soaking in the feel of him. Melissa had missed him so much, but until that moment Miles hadn't realized how much he'd missed him, too, how much he would miss them both when they were gone. They'd been playing this game of make-believe for so long and he'd become invested in it and in them. But it was time to reunite this family— and remind himself that he wasn't a part of it.

He glanced back to Ellie, who'd fallen to her knees in hysterical tears. He left the Dallas PD to handle her and carried Dylan outside to his truck.

Lanie approached him and Miles turned to her. "Thank you for coming when I needed you."

She gave him a half-hearted shrug. "Always." Then she punched him—hard—in the arm. "And that's for thinking I could ever be a mole or betray a witness. My aunt loaned me the money to buy that house."

He rubbed his arm. She was petite but fierce. "I'm sorry about that. I suppose Griffin told you about Adam, though?"

He saw a mixture of hurt and anger flash across her expression before she regained control of her emotions. "He did. After talking to Griffin, I went to Adam's apartment and did some snooping of my own. Apparently, he's been gambling. He's got debts."

Miles knew where this was leading. "And Max Shearer just happened to buy those debts."

She nodded. "Looks that way. I'll take my car and follow you back to the Silver Star to drop this little guy back with his mama, then we need to work on finding Adam before he does any more damage."

Miles buckled Dylan into his car seat, then he and Josh headed back to the ranch with Lanie, Griffin and three other marshals following behind. He phoned the house to let Melissa know and his mother answered. She squealed at the news. "She's resting upstairs. I'll run up there now and tell her."

He thanked her, then ended the call. At least he would be able to fulfill one promise he'd made to Melissa. He was returning Dylan to her. That would have to be enough to make up for his falling down on the job of keeping them safe in the first place. Then they would find Adam and bring him to justice, and send

Melissa and Dylan on to their new life and new identities with the assurance that the leak in WITSEC had been taken care of.

A crash shook the house and jerked Melissa awake. She'd been struggling to rest but must have finally dozed off. Now this.

She heard voices rising from downstairs, so she opened the door and rushed out. A few steps down, she saw what had made the jarring noise. A full-size SUV had slammed through the front window of the house.

She hurried down a few more steps before she saw bodies on the floor—Paul, John and Diane, all lying unconscious. Kellyanne was kneeling over Paul, then she looked up at the intruder. "You hit my brother. He was standing by the window."

John pushed himself to his elbows then tried to scramble to his feet. "Get out of here," he cried at the intruder, who didn't seem bothered in the least by his warning.

John lunged at the man, who used the back end of his gun to club him over the head. John grunted and fell back down, causing Kellyanne to rush over to him.

"Daddy, are you okay?"

Melissa started to turn and run back upstairs to phone for help, but the man's voice stopped her cold. "There you are."

She turned and saw his eyes locked on her. "Come here, Melissa. You're coming with me."

Fear locked her in her spot. She recognized him

as the man, the marshal, who'd given her back her mother's necklace. The man who'd bugged it and used it to track her to Courtland County and the Silver Star Ranch, all so he could hand her over to be murdered. She shook her head. "I won't go with you."

His face contorted and he reached for Kellyanne, pulling her to him as she cried out. He took his gun and pointed it at Kellyanne's head. "Come with me or I kill this woman."

Melissa took several steps down. "Okay, okay. Please don't hurt her."

Kellyanne's eyes were full of fright, but Melissa could still see her silently begging Melissa not to go. But Melissa had no choice. She couldn't allow this family to suffer any more because of her. Paul and John both definitely needed a doctor. She couldn't see Diane well enough to see what her injuries were, but she hadn't gotten up and that couldn't be a good sign. Once they were gone, Kellyanne could phone for help.

Besides, going with this man would lead her to her son.

She walked to the bottom of the staircase and stood to face him. "Miles is on to you," she told him.

He shoved Kellyanne away and reached for Melissa, pulling her against him and pressing the gun into her stomach. He sneered. "Then we'd better go before he gets home."

He pushed her into the front seat of the SUV, then

climbed in beside her, started the engine and backed away.

As he drove, she looked back with a sinking feeling that she would never see the Silver Star or the Avery family again.

TEN

They were a half hour away from the Silver Star when Miles received a phone call. He glanced at the screen and saw it was from the house phone at the ranch. He put it on Speaker. "Hello?"

"Miles?" Kellyanne's voice was high-pitched and strained. "Miles, a man broke into the house. Paul and Mom are hurt, and Dad—"

"I'm fine," his father grunted in the distance.

Josh's jaw clenched. "We're on our way back. We'll be there in twenty minutes."

He was worried about Paul and his parents being injured, but the fear in Kellyanne's voice had him shaking and he couldn't help noticing the name she hadn't mentioned. "Where's Melissa?"

Kellyanne broke into a sob and Miles's heart sank. "He took her! He took her, Miles, and we couldn't stop him." She broke down and ended the call.

Miles glanced at Dylan already soundly sleeping in the back seat. He'd finally brought him back to Melissa and now she was gone, too. Would this nightmare never end?

Josh turned on his lights and sirens and floored the accelerator. Miles phoned Lanie and Griffin to update them, and they kept up with Josh as they headed back to the ranch, making good time and arriving soon after the ambulance and Cecile. She met them as they parked and gave a rundown as Lanie and Griffin fell in behind them. But Miles didn't need a summary to understand what had happened here. The big, gaping hole in the front of the house said enough.

"It looks like Paul was standing in front of the window when an SUV crashed through it. He's suffered multiple injuries, including a broken leg, and has already been transported to the hospital. Your father received a gash on his head, but the paramedics were able to close it. He's refusing to go to the hospital, as is your mother, who had a blow to the head that left her unconscious for a few minutes. Kellyanne was shaken up, but suffered no serious injuries. She's the one who called for the ambulance."

Miles stood and stared at the house, which was a shambles, and at his family, who were all in pain. Anger burst through him that Adam, someone he'd considered his friend, had created such havoc. And now Adam had Melissa and was going to hand her over to a killer.

He turned to Lanie and Griffin and struggled to keep his composure. "We need to find Adam."

Lanie agreed. "I've been thinking about that since we left Dallas. I tried to access the GPS on his cell phone and his car, but both have been disabled. No surprise there. He's too smart to leave them on when he knows we're looking for him. However, when I was in his apartment, I found papers listing a cell phone that isn't his number. I'm thinking if it's a secondary phone he uses for his betting, he may not have thought to turn off the GPS on it since he wouldn't expect us to know about it to trace it. I may be able to access it and track his location."

Griffin nodded. "Get started on that."

Lanie pulled her laptop from her shoulder bag and set it up using the hood of the truck as a desk.

Miles pulled Dylan out of his car seat and carried him into the house. His parents and Kellyanne were sitting at the kitchen table and when she saw Dylan, Kellyanne hurried over and pulled him from Miles's arms. "I'm so glad you found him."

"Would you take him upstairs and put him to bed? He's had a long day." She agreed and hurried up the stairs.

Miles kneeled beside his parents. His mother was pressing an ice pack against the back of her head and his dad was sporting a large, bloody bandage. "We tried to stop him," his dad told him. "We tried to stop him."

He hugged them both, then suggested they go to the hospital. "Someone needs to be with Paul. Keep us updated."

They finally agreed, but as his mother stood, she hugged him again. "What are you going to do?"

He wanted to reassure her that everything was going to be fine. That he was going to find Melissa and bring her home and everything would be great, but he couldn't. He was scared. She was out there some-where and he had no idea how to even begin to find her. "I've got my team with me," he said, motioning to his brothers and Lanie and Griffin outside.

His mom must have seen his hesitation because she touched his face. "You can do this, Miles. You will find her and you'll bring her back to the Silver Star, where she and Dylan belong."

He hugged his mother tightly, then sent them on to the hospital. He wasn't worried about leaving Kellyanne and Dylan here at the house. Besides the police pres-ence investigating the scene, the danger to Dylan was over. No one was coming after him any longer. Adam had the person he wanted.

He walked back out to the car to check on Lanie's progress with renewed energy. He wasn't going to let Adam win. He was going to find Melissa and bring her home where she belonged—with him.

Adam gripped the steering wheel with one hand as he drove, keeping the gun trained on Melissa. She knew her best chance was to play it cool and look for an opportunity to escape before they got to wherever they were heading. But she couldn't, not until he took her to Dylan. Plus, she couldn't get past the fact that this man had betrayed Miles and an entire agency he'd taken an oath to. She couldn't make herself keep quiet about it. If she was going to die, she was also going to demand answers.

"Why are you doing this? What have I ever done to you?"

His voice was flat, emotionless, as he responded to her. "You haven't done anything to me. This isn't personal. I have no choice."

"You're the leak in the marshals service. You're the one who's been giving my location to Kirby and Shearer. And the attacks against me. That was all you?"

"Kirby was in hiding, so he and Shearer tasked me with taking care of you. I couldn't get too close either, or Miles might have spotted me, so I put the word out to the local teens. Some of them got a little out of hand."

"One of them nearly killed my son by placing him into a corral with spooked horses."

He shot her a regretful look. "I'm sorry about that. They got a little too aggressive trying to create chaos in order to grab you, but you jumped into the pen."

She touched the cast on her arm. She'd survived that incident but she might not survive this. "I thought you were being nice to me when you gave me back my necklace, but you were really tracking me the entire time."

"You don't understand. I have no choice. If I don't hand you over to them, they'll kill me."

"And what about my son? Where is my son?" She lost her cool as she kept screaming the question. This man and his accomplices had taken Dylan and now they had her, too. The screaming startled him so much that he lost control of the car and swerved. He swore, then shoved her backward in her seat.

"Don't do that again." His tone was hard and firm, but she wasn't afraid of him. If it meant getting her son back, she would do whatever it took.

"I want to know where my son is."

"I don't know where your son is. I didn't have anything to do with his abduction." She didn't see any signs of deception in him, but someone had taken Dylan.

"Then Shearer took him. I know he did."

"Shearer doesn't need to be kidnapping kids to get whatever he wants."

She leaned back in her seat and realized for the first time that he wasn't a part of the kidnapping of Dylan. Then where was her child?

Oh, God, please let them find him.

He would be safe with Miles if they did. She believed the Averys would take care of him—because she doubted she would be returning to him. This man was about to hand her over to a killer—the same killer who'd murdered her mother and had plans to do the same to her.

"Don't worry," Adam stated. "If he's out there, Miles will find him and take care of your son. He's a good guy."

"He's a good man who you stabbed in the back. He was almost killed in some of those attacks against me, you know. How could you betray your friends this way? Betray the people you'd sworn to protect?"

"Look, you don't know my life. I've gotten in over my head with some bad people. I had no choice but to comply. They wanted information. I gave it to them. They wanted you…"

"And you'll give me to them. Never mind that they'll kill me. At least, your debts to them will be paid." She couldn't control the contempt she felt for this man, or the way it manifested in her tone.

"What am I supposed to do? Just let them kill me? I don't want to die."

"Neither do I," she said, but she suspected that was exactly what was going to happen.

His cell phone rang and he glanced at the screen in the cradle on the dash. "It's Miles. They're probably looking for you by now." He glanced at her. "If I pick up, they won't be able to track the call, you know."

She gulped as she realized he was going to answer it and saw the truth in his face. He was giving her a chance to say goodbye.

He wiggled the gun to remind her he had it before he answered. "Hello."

Instead of Miles, she heard a woman's voice through the speaker. "Adam, what are you doing?"

"Hey, Lanie. What's up?"

"*What's up?* You just kidnapped Melissa, didn't you?"

"I really can't talk about that right now."

"You don't have to do this. I know what they have on you. The gambling debts. That's why you're doing this, isn't it?"

"I'm sorry," he said. "I never meant to hurt anyone. I never meant for this to happen. I had no idea who was holding my markers."

"Come back to the ranch. Bring Melissa back here safely. We can figure this out. We can place you in protective custody."

Melissa watched him and saw real regret in his face. He wanted to do what Lanie had asked, wanted to turn around and make this all right. And for a moment, she hoped that this woman's words had gotten to him.

But then he laughed. "You don't really believe I would be safe, do you?"

"I'll handle the protection myself. No one else would know."

He shook his head. "I used to wonder what would make all those people we've protected decide to turn on their friends. I always wondered what kind of person did that. Now, I guess I know. They were just looking out for themselves. Same as me."

"I guess that's true, but you don't have to do it."

Someone grabbed the phone, then Miles's voice came on the line. "Adam, where is Melissa?"

Adam gave her a look. "She's here. She can hear you." He nodded, giving her permission to speak.

"Miles, it's me. I'm here."

"Are you all right? Has he hurt you?"

Hearing his voice was like a balm to her soul and she started to cry. "I'm okay...so far." She heard the frustration and angst in his voice and longed to reassure him, but she didn't know how. She was in serious trouble. "The good news is that I don't think he had anything to do with kidnapping Dylan."

"Dylan is fine. We found him."

Relief flooded through her at those words. To know her son was okay made all of this a little more bearable. But tears pressed against her eyes at the realization that she would never get the chance to hug him again or tell him she loved him. "I'm sorry," she told Miles. "I shouldn't have lashed out at you the way I did.

It wasn't your fault and I knew it wasn't. I was just so angry and upset."

"I know. Don't lose hope because I'm not going to lose you, Melissa. We're not going to lose you. Dylan and I need you. Where are you?"

Adam grabbed the phone and ended the call. She cried out in anguish. He'd said *they* needed her. He needed her. She was done fighting it—she wanted to be with Miles. She wanted to be in his arms, where she felt safe and loved, and she wanted him to be a father for Dylan. Nothing else mattered.

Adam rolled down the window and tossed out the phone. "If I know my team, they'll keep trying to call and doing whatever they can to attempt to track us." With that action, she felt her last hope of being located evaporate. At least she'd gotten to hear Miles's voice. At least she'd gotten to learn that her son was safe. Adam had been right about one thing. Miles would take care of Dylan. The entire family would be there for him and he would grow up with a family who doted on him. She could at least take comfort in knowing that Dylan would finally have the life she'd always wanted for him.

Adam turned onto a dirt road, then pulled up next to an unoccupied parked car. He opened the door, grabbed her arm and pulled her out. They walked to the car and he used a set of keys to open the trunk. He took out duct tape and grabbed her wrists, wrapping the tape around them.

Fear rustled through her. This was it. He was readying her to hand her over to a killer. "Please, you don't have to do this. You heard Miles and that woman. They can help you. They can protect you."

He ripped off another piece of tape and shook his head. "I'm sorry." He slapped the tape over her mouth then shoved her into the trunk. She couldn't speak but her eyes kept pleading with him not to do this right up until the moment he slammed the trunk shut and darkness enveloped her.

He'd tied her up like a Christmas turkey ready to be handed over for slaughter. All that was left was the hand-off and there was nothing she could do to stop him.

She was going to die.

Melissa had no idea how long of a drive it would be, but after several moments of self-pity, she'd decided she was not going quietly. If she was going to die, she was going to fight back the same way she was certain her mother had. These people would not make her child an orphan so easily.

Still, she knew that her chances of survival were low. She couldn't survive this without help and she knew Miles might not make it to her in time. Her only hope, the only solace she had left, was in Jesus. She would probably be seeing Him soon and she was scared, so scared, not of dying because she knew Heaven and her mom were waiting for her, but for what she was leaving behind. Dylan…and Miles. She wished for more time, for different circumstances between them. If only she'd met him years ago before this nightmare had started. But there was little point in looking back and wondering what might have been. She couldn't change anything that happened—not the horrible parts, like losing her mother, or the wonderful parts, like meeting Miles. If she had to die, she would cherish the time they'd spent together, remember the feeling of being in his arms, the warmth of his embrace and the spark of his kiss. She wanted more. God knew she wanted more, but that was never going to happen. She was going to die without Miles ever knowing how much she loved him.

God, please take care of both Miles and Dylan. They're going to need You and each other to get through their grief.

The car stopped and she heard Adam getting out. She frantically pulled at the binds on her hands as footsteps neared the trunk. This was it. Her last moments. Horror and anguish pelted through her as footsteps approached the car.

Her time had run out.

Miles was glad Lanie was remaining calm and collected as she drove because hearing Melissa's voice had shaken him to the core. Sure, he'd gotten Dylan back, but he couldn't lose her now. Anger burned inside him—anger that his friend would do something like this to him, to any witness, but especially to the woman Miles had fallen in love with.

"I owe you an apology," Lanie said, wiping away a tear that made Miles realize she, too, was struggling to hold her emotions in check. "I've suspected something was going on with Adam for a while. He's gotten so moody and he disappears for hours at a time. I was too quick to dismiss it as nothing serious."

He'd overlooked the signs, too. "In our profession, it's easy to claim work as an excuse for seeming anxious or run-down."

"And he did. I should have listened to my gut. It was telling me something was wrong. Maybe I could have helped him before he got in this deep."

"This is not your fault, Lanie. Adam made his own choices."

"Isn't that what I always tell myself about our witnesses? They made their own choices. I always thought maybe they deserved what they got. But it seems like they made the choices and it's their families that have to pay the price."

He grimaced. "Now Melissa is having to pay the price for Adam's choices."

"It's not fair," she declared.

He looked at her. "Life's not fair. If it was, we would be out of a job." It was something they'd said to one another often when the weight of their work and all they had to witness got too much. But it was true. If real justice existed in this world, the bad guys would be punished for their actions and no one else would have to suffer. But sin meant that this world was often unjust and unfair. Only Jesus made everything right again. He held on to that. God was watching over Melissa and he was praying fervently for her, as he knew his family was, too. But was it enough? Would God honor those prayers? He knew sometimes the answer was no. God allowed bad things to happen because He'd given us free will. Right then, Melissa was paying the price for Adam's free-will choices.

Lanie continued to track the secondary cell phone. She'd purposefully called Adam on his primary phone, so as not to alert him they knew about the secret phone, which was still giving them directions to his location. He'd turned off the highway close to where an old feed-supply store used to be. The building had been abandoned since Miles was a kid. The perfect place to hide out or make a prisoner exchange.

Lanie pulled up behind a cluster of trees and they got out. Josh and Griffin and their respective teams were following behind. Lanie pointed to a silver sedan parked in front of the building, along with several SUVs.

"That's Adam's car."

Miles recognized it, too. It wasn't the SUV he'd used to smash through Miles's family home. He must have abandoned that vehicle and switched to his own.

Lanie kneeled down. "I'll try to get close and scope out who is inside, then we'll work out a plan."

She checked her weapon and stood, but Miles quickly grabbed her arm and pulled her back down as the door to the feed store opened and Adam emerged from the building.

"He's coming out."

Adam walked to his car, opened the trunk and pulled something out. Miles gasped when he saw Melissa being dragged from the trunk. It took everything inside him not to run to them right then and pound Adam into the ground for stuffing her into that trunk. Lanie touched his arm and he glanced at her, reading the meaning in her expression. He would have the opportunity to make Adam pay for his actions. He just had to hold on.

The door to the building opened again and several men walked out, including Richard Kirby, along with two men who looked to be his protection detail. So he had definitely been in town, although Miles suspected Adam had been the one behind recruiting kids for the attacks. It was more his style. Kirby would have just killed Melissa without all the fuss and drama. And he doubted a professional hitman actually needed a security detail. Either way, Miles was certain these men tied back to Shearer in some way.

Adam dragged a bound-and-gagged Melissa toward the group. He shoved her to her knees in front of Kirby. "There she is. Now, I want those assurances that my debt is paid."

Melissa's eyes were full of terror and Lanie had to touch his arm again to calm him. "Not yet," she whispered. He nodded his understanding, but it took every ounce of willpower he had to keep from reacting.

Kirby kneeled and stared at Melissa. He seemed to be studying her. Then he stood and pulled out his cell phone. "You did good." He pressed a button on the phone, then placed it to his ear. "It's her, boss. The woman who can identify me. Your guy in the marshals office finally came through for us." He paused for several moments, then nodded. "I understand." He ended the call, then slipped the phone back into his pocket. "Mr. Shearer thanks you for your assistance. He'll call you when he needs you again."

"No!" Adam stiffened and pulled out his gun, pointing it at them. "I was promised that if I took care of her, my debts would be cleared. I'm through. I'm done being ordered around by you or Max Shearer or anyone else."

Kirby rolled his eyes. His tone was sharp and biting when he responded to Adam's demands. "You are done when we tell you you're done. Not before." He made a motion and one of the muscle men grabbed Adam and shoved him to the ground next to Melissa.

Kirby reached into his pocket and pulled out his own gun. Miles's heart sank. He was going to kill her right then and there. It was time for them to act before it was too late.

Lanie raised her weapon and motioned for her team to move in. "US Marshals. Nobody move!" she yelled as the team sprang into action and surrounded the group.

Miles ran toward them, his gun trained on Kirby. "Put the gun down! Put it down!"

But all three men reached for their guns and began firing. Kirby turned his weapon toward Miles and fired. Miles returned fire and a shootout ensued. Melissa screamed beneath the tape covering her mouth and sprawled out on the ground. He prayed she stayed down and wasn't hit.

He shot Kirby several times—shots meant to disable, not to kill—before the man went down. He fell to the ground, but managed to raise his hands in surrender. "Okay, okay. I give up. You win."

The other two men were already on the ground and the deputies ran to surround them.

Miles hurried toward Melissa, but before he could

reach her, Adam grabbed her and picked up a gun, pointing it at Melissa's head as he dragged her toward the building.

"Don't come another step, Miles, or I'll kill her."

Miles fought to remain calm despite the way his heart hammered against his chest. He couldn't let Adam see his desperation and rage. He had to remain calm if he didn't want this matter to escalate.

"You don't want to hurt her, Adam."

"I don't want to, but I will." He backed up. "Now you're going to tell your people that we're getting into my car and driving away. Once I'm out of danger, I'll drop her off somewhere. I won't hurt her. I promise."

Miles trained his gun right between Adam's eyes. It wouldn't be an easy shot to make and there was a real risk that he might hit Melissa instead, but there was no other shot he could take. Adam knew what he was doing. He was using her as a shield very effectively. It would have to be a head shot and that was dangerous to Melissa, too.

Adam grinned at him the same way he had a hundred other times. He knew what Miles was thinking, always believed he could predict the way Miles's brain worked. "You won't risk it, Miles. Face it, you're not that good of a shot. I've been on the shooting range with you, remember." He pressed the gun into her face. "You won't risk taking it, not with this one. You won't risk hurting her."

He was right, but that didn't mean he'd won. Miles wasn't alone. He had a team of people that included his brothers and Lanie. Adam wouldn't leave here with Melissa. Even if Miles couldn't get a shot off, the people with him wouldn't fail him. It was the reason he'd come here to the sanctuary of his home, where he knew for certain his brothers would have his back.

Adam laughed. "I'm not the only one who broke the rules, you know, Miles. You did, too. We're not supposed to get emotionally involved with the witnesses, but I think you did, didn't you?"

Adam was trying to bait him, to force him to lose his focus, but that wasn't going to happen. Still, he couldn't refute his former friend's words. "You're right, Adam. I did break the rules. I fell in love."

"See! You're not so perfect, Miles."

"I never said I was perfect, but I'm not the one with a gun to a witness's head."

Adam stepped backward, heading closer to the car. He dragged Melissa with him. Miles briefly took his eyes off Adam long enough to see the fear in her expression. He tried to silently reassure her that everything was going to be okay. But was it? He didn't know. Adam had the upper hand when he had Melissa as his hostage and he'd already crossed more lines than Miles would have believed he was capable of. His friend was gone, and only an enemy stood in front of him. Adam had already taken away Miles's sense of family at the marshals service and his confidence in his team. Miles wasn't going to allow Adam to take this from him, too. He wouldn't allow him to take Melissa. Not when she was this close to him. He couldn't lose her now, not now.

God, please guide my actions.

"Adam, please don't do this. We can work this out. Just let her go and you can walk out of here."

"Now why don't I believe you?" Adam asked.

He knew Melissa was his only leverage and he wasn't walking away—or driving away—unless it was in handcuffs.

"I've never lied to you."

"That's not true," Adam demanded. "You lied when you said you were coming home to take care of your father. He wasn't sick. You didn't trust us. Why should we trust you?"

"My job was to protect the witness from a leak in the agency—from you. I did my job."

"I thought we trusted one another. Guess that was another lie."

He didn't flinch. "It's the job, Adam. If you can't handle it then you should have moved on."

"You know what this job does to you, Miles? It makes you realize that no one can really be trusted."

He didn't want to hear excuses. There wasn't one. "Let her go." But Adam wasn't listening. He was trying to work out a way to survive.

Miles was going to have no choice but to shoot him.

"Adam, stop this," Lanie demanded from behind Miles. She, too, had her gun trained on Adam. "You know how this is going to end. Don't force our hand." She lowered her gun, then put it away and took a step toward Adam, but not far enough so that she was in the line of fire. Miles realized what she was doing. She was distracting Adam, trying to throw off his concentration so that even if he didn't surrender, at least he might loosen his grip on Melissa.

Miles had missed his partner and was glad she had his back.

Miles locked eyes with Melissa while Lanie had Adam preoccupied. He needed her to fight and tried to silently send her that message. She needed to fight off Adam the same way she'd fought to survive all this time. Who else could have escaped an assassin's aim and a mob boss's wrath?

She nodded her understanding and started to struggle against Adam, squirming and jerking until she finally loosened his hold enough to slip through and fall down.

Before Adam could react, Miles shot, hitting Adam in the neck and sending him to the ground.

Melissa crawled away, while Lanie hurried over to Adam to check for a pulse. She looked at Miles and shook her head, indicating she didn't find one. "He's dead."

Miles put away his gun and hurried to Melissa, pulling the tape from her mouth. He helped her to her feet and cut the tape from her hands. Once free, she threw her arms around him and he pulled her close. "I thought I'd lost you," he said as a wave of relief knocked the wind out of him. Tears streaked her face and he wiped them away with his finger before he kissed her. "I love you, and I don't want to lose you."

She leaned into him. "I love you, too, Miles, and I don't ever want to lose you, either."

He kissed her long and hard, but refused to release her, even to walk to the car. "Let's go home," he whispered.

Christmas Eve turned out to be another mild and sunny day and Melissa agreed to let Lawson and Bree—who'd returned home early from their trip to learn about all that had happened—and Kellyanne put Dylan on one of the horses. Lawson reassured her that he'd made certain the mare was calm and that they would all be right there with Dylan as he rode around the corral.

She smiled at her son's laughter and felt sad again that she'd soon have to leave this place. They'd found refuge here…and so much more. She didn't want to go.

She turned and saw Miles still on the porch, phone to his ear. He was talking to his supervisor about her case. She had been glad to learn that the ranch hands Miles's brothers were mentoring hadn't been involved in any of the attacks against her, but several local college kids had been charged for doing Adam's dirty work and targeting her and Dylan. After being arrested, Kirby had immediately begun bargaining for a deal. He was willing to plead guilty and testify against Shearer. And, according to Miles, the US Attorney's Office was ready to make that trade. Kirby's guilty plea meant that Melissa wouldn't have to testify against him, which also meant there was a chance she wouldn't have to remain in witness protection.

The thought of returning to the home she'd shared with her mother saddened her. Nothing was left for her there. Everything she wanted was right here with Miles.

He'd told her he loved her and she'd said the same to him, but what did that mean for them now? It was easy to love him, but could she ever truly trust a man who could never share all of his life with her?

She'd been so sure that the answer to that question was no—but when she'd been held captive, she'd realized what truly mattered to her...and her answer changed. If that man was Miles, she could. She trusted him in a way that transcended everything else. When she'd been trapped in that trunk, she'd had no choice but to believe that God would protect her despite how distant He'd felt, and throughout this ordeal, He'd been with her, watching over her and guiding her to Miles. She trusted Him even without being privy to every detail of His plan because she knew He was a good and loving God.

She knew that about Miles, too—knew she could trust him implicitly with her life and with Dylan's. And if he had to keep things secret from her because of his job, she trusted him enough to understand and accept that.

He ended the call and slid his cell phone into his pocket as he headed toward the corral. She loved the way he walked and talked and kept an eye on her even while pretending not to. He leaned against the fence and waved to Dylan, who squealed with delight when Kellyanne walked the horse past them.

"That was Griffin. He says they've determined the threat against you has been neutralized. They don't believe anyone is coming after you anymore.

Shearer's network has been dismantled and you won't have to testify."

"So they're cutting us loose."

He nodded. "I agree with them. I've looked over the case and I don't think there's anyone left that wants to do harm to you or Dylan. There's no reason for it anymore. Kirby has taken a plea and he'll testify against Shearer, and the men in his circle are doing the same." He turned and look at her. "You're free, Melissa."

She sucked in a breath at the word *free*. She wasn't sure she even knew what it meant anymore. It had been so long since she'd felt true freedom. For too long, she'd been stuck in a rut, feeling trapped and caged. But she could go anywhere she wanted to go now and be anyone she wanted. She could finally give Dylan the life she'd always dreamed he would have.

She turned to Miles, then leaned in for a kiss. "I don't want to go anywhere, Miles. You've shown me what true freedom looks like, freedom in love and trust. How could I ever walk away from that?" She reached for his hand and wove her fingers through his. "I love you, Miles Avery, and I don't want to ever leave you."

His face broke into a smile and he pulled her close. "I was hoping you would say that. I'll turn in my notice to Griffin to transfer out of WITSEC this afternoon. I can't promise I won't travel in my new position with the US Marshals Service, but at least there won't be any secrets between us."

She shook her head. She hadn't expected him to give up his job. "I don't want you to leave WITSEC. That's not what I want."

"I don't care about it. I care about you. I love you."

"If you weren't in WITSEC, I know Dylan and I wouldn't be here today. You went above and beyond to keep us safe. I don't think we would have made it if we'd had another marshal. It's important for you to stay in WITSEC."

"I don't want to keep anything from you, Melissa. I want to be able to share anything and everything with you. I don't want there to ever be any secrets between us. I want you to trust me."

"I do trust you, Miles. If I've learned anything through this entire ordeal, it's that, even though I couldn't see God's plan, He was working for me all along. It's the same with you. I trust you, Miles, absolutely and completely. What Shearer and Kirby and even Adam Stringer meant for evil, God used to bring me to you. I trust Him. And I know that any secrets you keep from me won't be because you don't love me. I'll love you no matter what. And I want to be your wife and make a family with you."

He took her hands and held them. "Are you sure?"

She'd never been more certain of anything in her life and she told him so.

"In that case, will you make me the happiest man alive and marry me, Melissa?"

"Yes, I will marry you, Miles Avery."

He let out a whoop and lifted her up, spinning her around as happiness bubbled up through her.

Dylan squealed again and Kellyanne cheered. Then Melissa and Miles turned to see Kellyanne, Dylan, Bree and Lawson watching them, smiles plastered on their faces.

"Does this mean you really are going to be my sister?" Kellyanne called, and Melissa smiled and leaned into Miles.

"It does."

She closed her eyes and silently thanked God for finally bringing her all he'd ever wanted—a husband, a home and a family that loved her and Dylan.

* * * * *

Be sure to read the first book in Virginia Vaughan's Cowboy Lawmen miniseries, Texas Twin Abduction, *available now from Love Inspired!*

Dear Reader

Thank you for joining me for Miles and Melissa's journey! I am enjoying writing this new series and this book was no different. I loved the idea of pitting a heroine with trust issues with a man whose job it was to keep secrets. In the end, Melissa learned that the trust she had in Miles had less to do with what he did than who he was.

Like my characters, I've had to learn that trusting God doesn't rely on what He gives me or what He does or doesn't allow to happen in my life. I trust in the Lord because of who He is—Savior, provider, loving father and so much more.

I love to hear from my readers! You can reach me online at my website, www.virginiavaughanonline. com, or follow me on Facebook at www.Facebook.com/ ginvaughanbooks.

Blessings!
Virginia

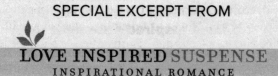
Sasha Eastman had never been afraid to stand on a
crowded street corner in Sheepshead Bay, New York.
She knew the ebb of city life—the busy, noisy, thriving
world of people and vehicles and emergency sirens. Since
her father's death two years ago, she found the crowds
comforting. She'd lost her mother at fourteen years old,
lost her ex-husband to another woman after three years
of marriage. She'd lost her father to cancer, and she had
no intention of losing anyone ever again. Being alone
was fine. She had always felt safe and content in the life
she had created.

And then *he'd* appeared.

First, just at the edge of her periphery—a quick
glimpse that had made her blood run cold. The hooked
nose, the hooded eyes, the stature that was just tall enough
to make him stand out in a crowd. She'd told herself she

was overtired, working too hard, thinking too much about the past. Martin Roker had died in a gun battle with the police eighteen years ago, shortly after he had murdered Sasha's mother. He was *not* wandering the streets of New York City. He wasn't stalking her. He wouldn't jump out of her closet in the dead of night.

And yet, she hadn't been able to shake the anxiety that settled in the pit of her stomach.

She had seen him again a day later. Full-on face view of a man who should be dead. He'd been standing across the street from the small studio where she taped her show. She'd walked outside at dusk, ready to return home after a few hours of working on her story. She'd been looking at her phone. When she looked up, he had been across the street.

And now…

Now she was afraid in a way she couldn't remember ever being before. Afraid that she would see him again; worried that delving into past heartaches had unhinged her mind and made her vulnerable to imagining things that couldn't possibly exist.

Like a dead man walking the streets.

Don't miss
Delayed Justice *by Shirlee McCoy,*
available wherever Love Inspired Suspense books
and ebooks are sold.

LoveInspired.com